DROWNING IN AIR

By

Judy Fitzwater

Judy Fitzwater

For Larry, Miellyn, and Anastasia,

Who share this adventure we call life with me.

This is a work of fiction. All characters and events described in this novel are fictitious or are used fictitiously.

Copyright © 2012 by Judith Fitzwater

Cover art copyright © 2012 by A. Brown

All rights reserved. This book, or any part of it, cannot be reproduced or distributed by any means without express permission in writing from the author.

Chapter 1

I can't breathe I can't breathe I can't breathe
I struggled upward from some deep descent.
I was drowning…in air.

Gasping, I forced air into my lungs. My ribs ached, and pain shot through my legs, which were threatening to crumple beneath me.

Slowly my eyes focused. Straight ahead of me was a stand of trees. And overwhelming my senses was the smell of gasoline.

Where was I?

Desperately I tried to slow my heart which was about to burst from my chest, but my legs gave way. I stumbled backward, realizing there was asphalt beneath my feet. My back hit something hard, and I spun around. It was a gas pump. I was at a gas station. I looked toward the bright lights to my right where a neon sign proclaimed I was at a 7-Eleven. Thank God, something familiar.

But it wasn't. As a cold sweat settled over me, I realized I'd never been to this gas station before. How could I have gotten here? I didn't see my Jeep. And I was completely alone.

Why was I here?

A car full of young men whipped into the lane, its horn blaring. I drew back, my legs like jelly, and grabbed onto the pump for support. I wanted to run, but my legs wouldn't work, I had no breath, and I didn't know where to go. The car made a U-turn back onto the road, and relief swept through me. I had to stay calm, so I could figure out what had happened to me. I *had* to stay in control. And the only way to do that was to clear my mind and figure out where I was.

But I could barely think. My head throbbed. I brought my hand up to touch my temple and felt something sticky all over it. I raised both of my palms into the light, and I saw blood. I felt my eyes widen in horror. Blood. All over my hands. I choked back panic and instinctively curled my fingers closed.

Had I been injured? Was that why I couldn't remember? I swallowed hard and forced myself to step into the bright light directly over the pumps, so I could catch my reflection in the chrome and see if I was hurt. I was shocked at the expression on my face, my gray eyes so frightened I barely recognized myself. But I saw no blood, not on my face, not matted in my long dark hair, not on my clothes.

But somehow I'd known instinctively, even before I looked, the blood wasn't mine. Someone had been badly hurt. I must have seen it.

Or had I been part of it? Laced with my fear was another emotion: guilt. Could *I* have hurt someone?

Bile rose in my throat and I swallowed hard, afraid I might throw up. I wanted the blood gone. I wanted it off of me. Now.

A spray bottle for cleaning windshields was in a nearby bin. Above it brown paper towels protruded from a dispenser. I grabbed them both and quickly scrubbed my hands, fighting back tears. When the blood was gone, I cleaned them again as though it were still there, wanting every trace, every speck off my skin. Then I cleaned the gas pump where I'd touched it and the spray bottle, and put it back. I disposed of the towels and the blood in the trash can, my hands shaking.

A breeze swept past me, and I shivered from the cold. I had no coat. My jeans and sweater were too thin for the night air, but the chill that ran through my heart had nothing to do with the weather.

Again, I looked about me. Something else was wrong. It couldn't be more than eight o'clock but the sky was midnight black. The lights were off inside the store. It was closed. That's why the car had made the U-turn and left. Everything except the gas pumps was locked up, including the little man in a booth, waiting to collect his money. I could see him eyeing me suspiciously. I stepped further into the shadows, hiding my face from view. But why? Why didn't I want him to see me? Why didn't I dare ask him for help?

What had I done?

Desperately, I searched my mind, hoping for some clue. The last thing I remembered was Wes Gallagher calling me about seven this evening, asking me to meet him at a bar in Dupont Circle in Washington, D.C. He'd made me so angry, like he frequently did, but he'd left me little choice. I'd put my driver's license, my cell phone, two twenty dollar bills, and one credit card into the pockets of my jeans, and grabbed my keys. I'd gotten into my Jeep, backed out of the driveway and headed toward the highway. And after that...

Nothing.

I felt the pockets of my jeans. My money, my phone, my license, and my credit card were all still there. But something else was there as well, wedged in my watch pocket. I looked down to see the glint of Dad's Distinguished Flying Cross, the one Wes had stolen the last time he was at my house, the one he'd promised to return if I'd come meet him.

So I had seen him. But where was he?

Yes, I'd been furious with him, but, God help me, surely I wouldn't have harmed him. Would I?

Why couldn't I remember?

I pulled the cell phone out of my pocket and wracked my fuzzy brain for Wes's phone number. I punched in several digits, hoping I had it right. It went directly to Wes's voice mail. "Call me," I pleaded and hung up.

Then I walked to the street signs at the corner of the station and hit 1 to dial Jackie Cortez's phone number.

"Pick up, pick up, pick up," I prayed out loud. "Please, just let her be home."

She answered on the second ring. "What's wrong?" Jackie asked, her voice twisted with sleep and worry.

"Nothing."

"Are you hurt?"

"No."

"Then why—"

"I'm stranded at a gas station somewhere in D.C." My voice cracked. "Jackie, I don't have my Jeep or my keys. Could you find the spare key to my house and come get—"

"Where?"

I gave her the names of the cross streets. She hung up before I could finish saying, "Please hurry."

"What the hell were you doing in downtown D.C. by yourself at one in the morning?" Jackie demanded.

"I don't remember," I mumbled.

"What do you mean you don't remember?"

"I bumped my head, and I got confused. That's all," I insisted, hoping she'd just let it go, but I knew better. Jackie, like me, never let anything go. But I could deal with my head later. At the moment, any injury to me didn't matter.

The only thing that did matter was that I was safe and someplace familiar. The car doors were locked, warm air was blasting, and heater coils were warming my rear, as we headed up Wisconsin Avenue out of the city. Maybe I could finally learn how to breathe again.

I stared out the window of her Mercedes coupe, hoping she wouldn't pick up on how truly shaken I was. We were good enough friends she shouldn't need answers, especially when I had none to give. But that wouldn't stop Jackie.

"I didn't drive all the way down here for you to give

me the silent treatment, Eva."

She must have heard the desperation in my voice because she'd made the trip from Potomac, Maryland, in record time. She'd found me huddled near the ice cooler at the side of the 7-Eleven, a few blocks off Dupont Circle in an area I don't remember ever having been before. Thank God she'd found me.

She actually took her eyes off the D.C. streets and looked at me. I could see the anger flash in her eyes. "Your phone call scared me half to death. I was afraid Luther Isaacs…"

"Had hurt one of us," I finished.

"Yeah. That's exactly what I thought."

"The man's only been out of prison a week."

"Yes. And it took him only one evening to murder eight people."

Silently I cursed the legal system. Isaacs had never been convicted of the drive-by shootings of those eight people, The August Eight, as the press had dubbed them. And now he'd been turned back onto the streets after serving his full sentence for felony theft, but not a single day for all of those murders fifteen years ago.

"He knows we all want him back in jail, especially you. Eva, I warned you not to make that documentary of yours." She shook her head. "You might as well put a sign on your back saying *Take your best shot*. What were you thinking being out late at night alone in the city?"

"I can take care of myself," I insisted.

"Right. That's why you wound up at a strange gas station with a bump on your head. Who hurt you?"

"I don't know. No one. I'm fine, Jackie, really," I said.

Jackie had always been protective of me. And now she was ready to tear apart anyone who might have laid a finger on me.

"Any scratches, bumps, or bruises I have will be gone

by morning, I promise. I'm sorry I had to get you out of bed in the middle of the night. And I'm sorry I scared you."

Jackie was the closest thing I had to a sister, and I loved her dearly. But I had no answers to the questions she asked.

She reached over and touched my hand, but I quickly drew it away. I didn't want her to feel it shaking beneath her own.

She let out an exasperated breath. "It'd be nice if you didn't hang out with psychopaths."

"I don't 'hang out' with psychopaths. The ones I interview are incarcerated."

"Right. That should make me feel better. Eva, you *invite* trouble."

"I do my job, Jackie." Now I was getting angry. "The documentaries I make are important. They not only increase awareness about the psychopathic mind, but, in at least two cases, I've been able to gather enough information to gain convictions."

And this one—the one I was working on now—was the most important. It was going to put Luther Isaacs back behind bars for good, if not buy him the death penalty.

"I'm not faulting what you do. I just wish you'd let someone else do it. You're going to get yourself killed. You have a degree in film from NYU for goodness sakes. You could make documentaries about other things."

"Funny you should mention that. I tried, remember? No one was interested. The public likes gore. That's where the money is."

Lots of money. Enough that I could concentrate on Isaacs and see that he was brought to justice, especially now that his release had renewed interest in the case.

"You didn't get that bump on your head all by yourself, whether you'll admit it or not," Jackie said. "How bad is it?"

"I told you, it's nothing," I insisted, forcing my voice to sound normal.

"If it was nothing, you'd know how you got to that gas station."

I could have a mild concussion, but I had no blurred vision, no nausea, and my confusion only had to do with my loss of several hours. But how I'd come by the bump, I had no idea. I was too afraid to even guess.

"I'm taking you to Suburban Hospital," she insisted.

"No!" I shouted, rising up as far as my seatbelt would allow. "You're taking me home."

"You need to see a doctor, and if you won't—"

"I will. Just not now. Please, Jackie, let it go. I'll be all right."

What I needed was to calm down enough to think. Maybe then I could remember. I'd had blood on my hands. I had to know what had happened before I tried to explain to anyone—especially the police who could tie me up for hours—how I'd wound up at a strange gas station in the middle of the night. I needed to know if someone had been hurt—if *I* could have hurt someone. If Wes was all right.

"Where's your Jeep?" Jackie asked.

I shook my head and looked at her, noticing for the first time how she was dressed. Only Jackie would have bothered to put on her copper studded designer jeans and a matching dark brown leather jacket the exact same color as her eyes to come get me in the middle of the night. It made me smile.

"I don't know where my Jeep is," I confessed.

"Okay, then where are your keys?"

"Ask me something I know and I'll answer you."

"Eva, what's going on?" she pressed, her words more gentle this time, hinting at how worried she really was.

"Take me home," I insisted again.

"With me? Damn straight."

"No, to my home."

"Then I'm staying with you."

"I'll be all right by myself. Besides, your husband will

want you home," I reminded her.

"So?"

Jackie's husband Rick was just back from a week's business trip to Reno. He missed Jackie when he was away, and he'd expect her to be there when he got up. He liked their weekends together. And he didn't particularly like me.

"Look, I need to be alone."

Jackie knew me well enough to understand that, even if she didn't like it. I could see her jaw set as she stared through the windshield, her regal face framed by long, curly hair, hair almost as dark as my own. I'm sure she thought I was lying, that I just didn't want to tell her what had happened. That was probably better than her believing I had amnesia.

"Conrad called my house looking for you. He wants you to call him back—if I should hear from you—as soon as possible. He sounded upset."

My producer had no business bothering Jackie just because I hadn't called him back right away. I was supposed to give him some raw footage of some of the interviews I'd already done. He needed to have them over the weekend so he could cue them up before he showed them to one of our backers Monday morning. He knew how important this project was to me, so he had to know I'd get him the footage in plenty of time.

I'd been only seventeen when my boyfriend was shot as I held his hand that August night and then watched his life's blood drain away as I cradled his head in my lap. David's death had shattered me. My youth and my innocence had died with him, and in their place had been born an anger and resentment I still struggled to control. And a new purpose in my life. His murderer had never paid for his crime, but he would. I'd see to it.

I shook off my thoughts and settled back into the leather of Jackie's Mercedes. I had nothing more to offer her right now. Because my last memory was of going to meet Wes

Gallagher who'd said we might have a break in the case, I knew that what had happened tonight was somehow connected to those murders fifteen years ago.

"Does this have to do with Wes?" Jackie asked as though reading my mind.

Her question startled me. "Why would you ask that?"

"Because he's the only person I know who would strand you at a gas station in the middle of the night."

Wes was a lot of things—self-absorbed, irresponsible, certainly undependable, and definitely unable to cope with a crisis. Sometimes he'd disappear for days. But I didn't believe he would abandon me if he thought I needed his help. And I didn't believe I would have hurt him, despite how angry he might have made me.

Jackie had never understood our relationship. I didn't expect her to. Her loss that night had been her father—not her first love. And she hadn't witnessed his death.

Wes and I had fallen irresistibly in lust when we were introduced at a support group for the August Eight families. He'd been nineteen. His girlfriend Sabrina had been one of the victims, shot on the sidewalk while on a smoke break at a dance at a community center—a dance she'd gone to without him. We'd been drawn to one another by our grief, by survivor's guilt, and by our need to feel alive again. Over the past fifteen years there had been times I'd wished I'd never met him. Sabrina's death had scarred him. David's had scarred me as well. We weren't good for each other, yet we seemed to have a bond Wes was determined to keep, and I couldn't completely break.

"Wes called me this morning, technically yesterday morning if you say it's two o'clock now. He's been working with me the past week because my cameraman's been sick."

"You know better than to let Wes work for you."

"He's good with a camera."

"Only because you trained him."

"Which means he knows my moods and how I work."

"And every button you've got to push." Her eyes flashed even in the dim light of the car.

"It was only one week, Jackie. I didn't want to get behind on the schedule, and it helps that Wes is familiar with what we're working on. We were filming at the site of the third murder."

She shot me a look, the one with the raised eyebrow. "Once Wes has an opening, he doesn't go away. You know that, Eva."

I did know that.

"And you know better than to feel sorry for him. How'd he get your phone number this time?"

"I have no idea."

Wes always found my unlisted phone number, even when I changed it, even through both of my marriages.

Jackie blamed Wes for the breakup of my first marriage, but she was wrong. His intrusions into my life could be annoying but they weren't unmanageable. I was perfectly capable of screwing up my own life.

I wondered sometimes what Wes would have been like if Sabrina hadn't died. It wasn't a fair question. I certainly wasn't who I would have been if David had lived.

"Was Wes hitting you up for money or just hitting on you?"

"He wanted more work."

But there'd been more that Wes had wanted. To make sure I'd listen to him when he called, he'd taken my father's Distinguished Flying Cross when he'd helped bring in my equipment into my house Friday afternoon. I'd kept it draped over Dad's military photo after he'd died last year.

Wes took it because he did things like that. He wanted a hold over people, only he'd used up his last emotional hold over me years ago. He delighted in the game of keep away whether he was teasing with his emotions or with some actual object. He took it because he knew I'd want it back and that would make me talk to him — when *he* wanted to talk to me — even when I didn't need him to work. I wasn't playing his game anymore. I would not be manipulated again.

But this time he'd called me back not once, but twice, talking both times to my answering machine, knowing full well I was home and listening to every word he said. He'd begged me to meet him that night in downtown D.C. at 8 P.M. at an address near Dupont Circle. He'd said it was important. Someone wanted to talk with me about something to do with the documentary. He'd said I'd be sorry if I didn't come, that we might have finally gotten a break in the case, that we might be able to get the evidence we needed to convict Sabrina and David's killer. Then he'd said he was sorry he'd taken the medal, that he'd give it back as soon as he saw me.

I've heard a lot of different emotions in Wes's voice over the years, but this was a new one. He'd sounded desperate.

Had we met with someone? Could it have been their blood on my hands? What the hell had happened tonight?

Jackie didn't seem to notice the panic I felt rising anew inside of me. I leveled my breathing. Only a few minutes more and I could cry or scream alone in the safety of my own home.

Jackie stared straight ahead as the car's headlights flashed up my street, her mouth set in a pout, still fuming that I'd seen Wes.

"Are you sure about this?" Jackie asked as she stopped in front of my double car garage, the engine idling.

I nodded, bringing myself back to the present. "Absolutely. I need some time alone. I *will* be all right."

"No more Wes?"

"No more Wes. My regular cameraman will be fine by tomorrow afternoon in plenty of time to start the week's filming," I assured her, my hand on the door lock.

"Tomorrow?" Jackie grabbed my forearm. "Eva, what

day is this?"

I stared at her.

"It's early Sunday morning. Why would you—"

Her brows were knitted, her lovely features contorted in concern. "Eva, it's early *Monday* morning."

"I'm too tired for jokes."

But her face remained strained and she didn't let go of my arm. "This is no joke. It's Monday."

"You're mistaken," I stated evenly.

"No, I'm not. Eva, where have you been for the last day and a half?"

Chapter 2

Jackie let out an indecipherable curse in Spanish, threw the transmission into reverse, and looked over her shoulder, ready to back out of the drive—with me still in her car.

"What do you think you're doing?" I protested, coming out of my seatbelt and unlocking my door. The shock that had come with realizing how much time I'd actually lost was ousted by a super dose of adrenaline and the need to be out of Jackie's car.

"What I should have done to begin with. I'm taking you to the hospital."

I jerked open my door.

"I was just mixed up, Jackie," I said, holding my voice amazingly steady considering the tumult inside of me. Thirty-two hours of my life were missing. Where the hell had I been for thirty-two hours?

"I'm fine," I repeated. "I'm going inside and I'm calling my own doctor."

I hated to lie to her, but I lived my life by trusting my instincts. I could not spend hours in a hospital emergency room or being grilled by police. I had to find Wes as soon as possible. He had to know what had happened during my missing hours—what I had done, where the blood had come from. And I had to make sure he was all right.

I also needed to get in touch with the private eye I'd hired to tail Isaacs since his release. If Isaacs had been anywhere near me, he would know.

Jackie was furious. If I didn't know she loved me, I might have mistaken that fiery look for hatred.

"Look at me," I insisted. "I'm rational and I'm not even

really hurt. I was just confused." I stared her down.

"You're calling your doctor?"

"Yes. I'm calling my doctor."

"And you're calling me as soon as you speak with him?"

"Go home, Jackie. I'll call you if I need you."

Indecision was written all over her face, but she hadn't been my best friend for fifteen years without learning something about me. Stubborn as she was, she knew which one of us was going to win this argument.

"Love you," I said.

"Love you back."

We said things like that, both of us always acutely aware we might not get a chance to say it again.

I stepped out of the car and stopped. Something wasn't right. I sensed it, even with the security lights blazing.

There was nothing I could put my finger on, and yet I could feel the hair rise on the back of my neck. But why? The front of my house looked perfectly normal. I'd had all the bushes removed from around the entrance, leaving nothing for anyone to hide behind. There were double locks on all the doors and a full alarm system covering every entrance and every window. Living with the memory of David's death and making my documentaries had made me paranoid. I lived alone and I needed to be able to sleep at night. My home was safe. If someone had tried to get inside, the alarms would be blaring and the police would already be here. I must simply be rattled from what I'd been through tonight.

"What's wrong?" Jackie asked.

"Nothing. I'm fine. My leg just cramped up," I lied, "but it's all right now." I shut the car door, convinced my paranoia had to be nothing more than exhaustion.

She rolled down her window and ordered, "Call me."

"I promise," I said and winked at her. Jackie, flashy as she might be, was the best. "Tell your husband he owes me one for sending you home."

She almost smiled. "You aren't *sending* me anywhere. You're throwing me out."

Jackie waited to leave until I unlocked my front door with the key she'd brought me. I stepped inside the entrance way, keyed in my alarm system, and felt the fear inside me ease. I was home where I was safe.

The foyer was a bit grandiose and not at all my taste: vaulted ceiling, black and white marble tile, a crystal chandelier hanging a couple of feet above my head. What can I say? The house was in a good area, not too far from Jackie's home, and it had proved an excellent investment.

I'd furnished the house with just enough pieces to get by, which gave it almost a model-home appearance. The thought made me laugh — me living in a model home. In truth, I pretty much used only the kitchen/sitting room area and the room across the hall, which was designed for an office but served as my bedroom. It was almost like living in an apartment within my own house.

I checked the alarm system again, tossed the key into a glass tray on a small table beside the door, and headed for the kitchen and some much needed orange juice. I flipped on the light, pulled open the door of the stainless steel fridge, grabbed the carton, turned around, and froze.

In front of the bank of windows that looked out onto my deck was a man resting comfortably in one of my rattan chairs. His feet, covered in black boots of heavy leather, were propped on a small wicker coffee table, and his head rested casually on his palms tucked behind his neck. His well developed biceps were in full view, one with some sort of tattoo. He was wearing a tight, black T-shirt, jeans, and a leather belt with a buckle the size of my fist.

"Hey, lover," he said in a low, inviting, possessive tone, "I was wondering if you were ever going to come home to me."

My heart stopped, and I almost dropped the juice. If I'd been in a crowded bar with friends, I might have been intrigued. But I was alone with this man in my home—my home, damn it, where I was supposed to be safe. I should have been afraid, but fear would do me no good. Instead, I was angry. I'd had one hell of a night, and I didn't need one more thing.

I tensed into defense mode and felt my eyes narrow. I had only myself to rely on. Jackie would already be out to the main road by now. And I had no way of signaling her anyway.

"What the hell are you doing here?" I demanded.

He dropped his arms and leaned forward. His face came into the light and my breath caught in my throat. He was tanned and ruggedly handsome, with thick, dark hair, and his skin had just enough lines around his eyes to make me believe he was in his mid-thirties. Damn. He was good looking. Even better than Wes.

He grinned with such familiarity that I felt my whole body react. Could he have mistaken me for someone else?

Not in my own house.

"That's some greeting, Evie, especially since you told me to meet you here. I brought your Jeep home, like you asked. It's in the garage."

I had never seen this man before in my life. Believe me, I would have remembered those smoky green eyes that held my gaze. But that was the point—I didn't remember. He, however, definitely seemed to know me. And for the moment, it might be better if I let him think I knew him, too, at least until I figured out what he wanted.

Behind me, on the counter, was a butcher block full of knives. The one in the back slot was specially weighted for throwing. I wasn't as defenseless as I looked. If he knew anything about me, he should know that, too.

I leaned my back against the granite and studied the

man. There was something about his demeanor...he seemed comfortable with me, almost as though he trusted me. But why would he?

I looked him over, trying not to get distracted by his obvious physical attributes. He didn't appear to be armed. He certainly wasn't hiding anything under that shirt. And he didn't seem menacing. Indeed, he seemed, well, friendly.

"You startled me," I said honestly.

"Sorry about that."

Slowly, he stood, stretching and flexing his substantial muscles as though he'd been sitting for a good while. His hands were empty. If he did have a weapon, it was probably in his boot, not that it mattered. He was much stronger than me.

"Want some juice?" I offered.

He shook his head.

I turned my back on him and quickly took a small glass from the cabinet, keeping an eye on his movements in the reflection of the chrome toaster. He stayed exactly where he was.

For the moment, I wanted him to think I was comfortable with him as well. I poured the juice, returned the carton to the fridge, and quickly turned to face him, again leaning my back against the counter, sipping the sweet liquid, the knife within easy reach.

Did he have my keys? He'd have to if he'd driven my Jeep home, but how had he gotten the code to my security system? He must have them both if he'd managed to get into my home without making a mess and setting off the alarms. No one else had either except for Jackie, and I had Jackie's key with me. Had I given them to him? How else could he have gotten them? But why would I put that much trust in a man I didn't know? I didn't trust many people I *did* know.

And how was I going to get him out of my house?

"Where's Wes?" I asked casually.

"You're the one who should know that," he said, taking a step toward me.

"Hold it right there," I warned, tensing as my heart sped up. I calmly set the juice next to me on the counter.

His eyes intensified as he stopped still. "Something wrong, Evie?"

"I prefer Eva."

Wes was the only person who called me Evie. So he probably did know Wes.

His face suddenly turned solemn and his eyes softened as he stared at my forehead. "You're hurt."

Instinctively I touched the bump with my hand. Why would this man care whether or not I'd been injured?

"It's nothing. I'm fine."

A smile curved the corner of his nicely defined mouth as he tossed my missing keys onto the counter.

So I *had* been with him—*if* he were telling the truth. He'd had my Jeep. At least he wasn't a thief.

Suddenly I realized what had been wrong when Jackie and I had pulled into the driveway. I must have seen the outline of my Jeep through the garage windows when nothing should have been there.

I grabbed up the key ring. It still had my pepper spray attached. I gripped it, my thumb poised to use it. Why would he arm me if he intended me harm?

"You weren't where you said you'd be," he said. "I waited almost two hours to pick you up. Then I came to the house."

Did he mean last night—during my missing hours? How long had he been here waiting in the dark. And why?

"About what happened last night..." I started, hoping he'd give me some clue.

He gave me a curious look, and I felt as if I were in some cat and mouse game with a most attractive and highly intelligent opponent. "What did happen, Eva?"

Enough. I was tired of playing this game. I didn't know this man, he was offering me no explanation I could make sense of, and I had no memory of inviting him into my house. If he was legit, I'd buy him a drink later and we'd have a good laugh. If not...

I gripped the pepper spray and drew in a quick breath. One move toward me and I'd take him down with the spray. I walked swiftly past him to the French door that opened onto the deck. All I had to do was flip the lock and open it. An alarm would go off and straight to the police station, and I would go straight outside into the woods.

As my hand touched the lock, I caught a flash of a reflection in the darkness outside near the trees.

Behind me my visitor shouted, "Get down!"

I ducked as the door and the windows beside it exploded. My companion was already in motion, diving toward me. We hit the floor together as splintered glass showered over us, his body blocking much of it as he tried to cover me. Alarms blasted throughout the house, and dozens of shards jabbed at my skin as I protected my head as best I could with my forearms. My breath was knocked from my chest, and I could feel every bruise on my body deepening.

I twisted beneath him and pushed against his chest. He eased his weight off of me, staying so close I could feel his warm breath across my cheek.

"You all right?" he whispered.

His scent was somehow familiar and oddly comforting. I'd been close to him before.

"I think so. You got a name?" I asked.

He looked at me as though I were nuts, his nose only inches from my own. "You knew it a few hours ago."

"Yeah, well my memory's not what it used to be."

"I was beginning to suspect as much. Simon Talbot."

"Eva Keller. Nice to meet you...again."

Simon gave me a narrowed look as he slid a 9 mm out of his boot.

"Cover your ears," he warned, and then he shot the bulb right out of the overhead light fixture.

"Hey! Do you have any idea how much that thing cost?" I demanded, the sound of the blast ringing in my ears.

But it had to be done. With the light on, we'd be on full display.

"Stay put," he ordered.

Obviously, he didn't know me well. I rolled away from him, shaking shards from my hair. I crouched as I crossed the glass strewn floor toward the hall and my bedroom. Simon didn't wait to see what I was doing. He was ahead of me on his way out the front door of the house. I had the feeling Simon, like me, wasn't about to let anyone get away with shooting at him.

At the door to the hallway, I stood and ran across into the dark of my bedroom. I grabbed a revolver out of the top drawer of my bedside table, my hand surprisingly steady against the grip, and scurried back through the house and out the front door. I came up behind Simon on the right side of the house. Security lights blazed across all the edges of the house, leaving us, and anyone else nearby, little shadow to hide in. If someone was out there, he was still in the woods.

Simon whirled on me, his gun in my face, his green eyes wide. "Don't do that! I could have killed you."

I shook my head. "I would have dropped you before you got a shot off."

He raised an eyebrow. "Oh, really."

"Yeah, really."

I'd probably had more training than he had. There's a private school in Pennsylvania. They teach just about everything anyone might want to know about weapons and how to use them. I'd wanted to know a lot.

"Is he gone?" I asked.

"I think so."

My breathing slowed, but I knew not to let down my guard. "Smart move. He was alone."

"How do you know that?" he asked, watching me closely.

"Because Luther Isaacs works alone."

Isaacs' name produced no reaction and no questions. So Simon knew who he was.

"The alarms should clue him in that the police are on their way," I continued. "Besides, the man's basically a coward."

"So you're convinced it was Isaacs? You think he was sending you a warning?" His eyes narrowed again, and I sensed that now he didn't completely trust me either.

"Nope. People don't warn you with shotguns. I think he intended to blow my head off. Maybe yours, too."

"Not likely mine. If he'd wanted me, he could have shot me while I was waiting for you to come home."

"You were sitting in the dark," I reminded him.

"True."

"Two for the price of one?"

"Now that's a possibility," Simon agreed. "You seem awfully calm for someone who was just shot at. Most people would be hysterical."

I *was* calm when I had to be, at least outwardly. I have a strange relationship with death. I've made a kind of uneasy peace with it. I know it can come anytime, but I wasn't ready to die yet, and I wasn't about to let Isaacs be the one to take me down.

It would have been different if somebody's life had been centered around my own. But I hadn't been in love for years. What's more, I intended to keep it that way. I had poor taste in men. Wes and my two exes were proof enough of that. Or at least that's what I told myself. Maybe I was just afraid of being in love, of having someone taken from me, someone I actually cared about. Or maybe I was afraid of leaving someone behind to mourn me. It's not the dying. It's the living that scares me.

And what I might have done to someone else. How had that blood gotten onto my hands?

"Just who the hell are you?" I demanded of Simon.

He didn't even try to hide his exasperation. "Simon—"

"No, I got your name."

"For Christ's sake, Eva, what the hell's wrong with you?"

I stared at him.

"Pittsburgh P.D.," he finally said. "I'm a detective."

I felt like I'd had a blow to my chest. What was a Pennsylvania police detective doing waiting for me in my home?

"Did you come here to arrest me?"

He frowned at me. "For what?"

"We don't have time for this." I motioned toward the backyard.

He gave me an exasperated look, but he knew I was right. "Wait here while I take a survey of the backyard," Simon said.

"Not on your life," I told him.

"You always this difficult?"

"You have no idea."

He shook his head, as though not quite sure what to make of me.

Together we circled around past the bushes and into the trees at the back of the lot. We heard nothing except the wail of the alarms from the house and now police sirens joining them in the distance. They'd be here any minute.

Near the base of a tall pin oak, Simon almost stumbled over what looked in the dark like a large garbage bag. He drew a small flashlight from his pocket, turned it on, and the blob took shape.

It was a man with a hole in the middle of a mass of dried blood that had soaked his shirt. I tried to lift his arm with the toe of my shoe, but his body was in rigor. I'd seen a lot of dead bodies in photos from my work, but this was my first up-close and personal, been-dead-awhile corpse. I was thankful most of it was hidden by the shadows.

"He's been dead several hours," I said.

"Do you recognize him?" Simon asked, shining the light across the body and then coming to rest on his face.

My heart almost stopped.

The man was white, slightly overweight, and middle-aged, with a close cropped, neatly trimmed beard. He was dressed in some sort of wool, long-sleeved shirt, a tan windbreaker and khaki pants.

"Yes, I know him," I managed, choking on my words. "His name is Albert Haggerty, and I'm the reason he's dead."

I was shivering now to the point that my teeth chattered. I hugged my arms around my torso, fighting to regain control. I was glad Simon couldn't see my face in the dark.

"He's...he's a private detective. I...I hired him to tail Luther Isaacs. He's been on the job since Isaacs was released from prison last week."

Simon passed the light briefly over my features and then moved closer. For a moment, I thought he might put his arm around me. Than he seemed to think better of it.

"I'd say he's lost track of Isaacs," Simon said.

"But I'll bet you Isaacs knows exactly where Haggerty is," I said.

Chapter 3

"Find Isaacs," I demanded.

"We intend to." The police officer who sat across from me was keeping his cool, which was more than I could say for myself. I looked again at my watch. It was almost eight o'clock in the morning, I was exhausted, and the dining chair I'd been sitting on for the last hour looked a whole lot better than it was comfortable.

"Do you know anyone else who might want to kill you?" he asked. He was younger than me, earnest, thorough, and wasting my time.

"Why would you even suspect anyone else?" I said evenly, hoping to disguise the frustration bubbling inside of me. "Al Haggerty was following Isaacs. *That's* why he was killed. I've already explained all of this to you. Call Al's wife. She knew his movements."

A wave of sadness swept over me as it again hit me exactly what Al's death would do to his wife Wilma. How would she cope? Al's death would devastate her.

I cleared my throat. "And call Jesse Sedwick."

"Detective Sedwick? He's retired."

"Tell *him* that. As far as he's concerned, the August Eight is still his case. He can fill you in on all of the details. You need to pick up Isaacs *now*, before he shoots someone else. He could be anywhere by now."

"We've already issued an APB for him."

That's all I needed to hear. I was more than ready to be away from my house. I still hadn't heard from Wes. If I thought it would do any good, I would have told the officer about my amnesia and the blood on my hands. But if I did, I could kiss the rest of the day good-bye, and it'd do nobody any good. I still needed to find Wes. He wasn't at home. If he had been, he would have returned one of the half dozen messages I'd left on his land line. And his cell phone was going straight to voice mail.

I wasn't ducking responsibility. I didn't know where to tell the police to look for Wes. And if it turned out I'd done something illegal — if I'd hurt someone — I'd be more than willing to confess to the police — once I found out what that something was. But until then...

I stood up. "Do you need anything else from me?"

He shook his head. "I think that about does it. Detective Talbot's account of the events pretty much agrees with yours, and Mrs. Cortez has confirmed by phone the time that she dropped you at your house."

"Good. You have my cell phone number if you need me."

He looked surprised. "You're leaving? You have an awfully big hole in your wall. You might want to do something about making your place secure before you go," he suggested.

"T. J. Contracting will be here within the hour. I assume you guys will be babysitting the place until they get here."

"We'll probably be here most of the morning."

"Right." The place would be crawling with cops all day and probably a good part of tomorrow. Another good reason for me to get out of the place.

Simon was leaning against the wall, one ankle crossed over the other, as I stepped into the hallway. I was sure he'd heard every word I'd told the officer.

"Ready?" he asked, standing up straight. He had to be exhausted, but he didn't look it. His eyes pierced right through me.

"For what?" I asked, returning his stare.

"To get out of here."

"Almost."

I dialed Jesse Sedwick's cell phone number, relieved when he didn't pick up. I left a message. "I'm all right" was all I said and then hung up.

Simon cocked his head. "Was that your significant other?"

"That was a message for a man who sometimes confuses himself with my father."

Simon didn't comment, but he didn't move either, and, for some reason, I found myself offering him an explanation.

"Jesse Sedwick helped the victims' friends and families get through the aftermath of the killings, especially Wes and me. He thinks he's family."

"And you think…"

"That he's overprotective. He doesn't want me doing my documentary on Isaacs. He's afraid it'll get me killed."

"I see. Could be he's right."

I slanted him a warning look and he let it go.

"What say we blow this joint," Simon suggested. "We could take your Jeep to my place."

I needed to know exactly what had happened between Simon and me during my missing hours, and he was the only one who knew. I didn't care where we went as long as it was somewhere Isaacs wasn't likely to look for us, and Simon's place shouldn't be on Isaacs' list.

"Not the Jeep, the Honda." No one would be able to follow us on the motorcycle.

So Simon and I donned our leather jackets and took off. He wanted to drive and I let him because it helped center our weight on the machine and I was still more shaken from being shot at and finding Al's body than I wanted to admit, even to myself. The wind felt good against my cheeks and on the back of my neck below my helmet. I leaned forward, giving in to the rush of speed, and wrapped my arms tighter around Simon's chest, enjoying the feel of his muscles beneath the leather. I rested my head against his back, as the two of us became one with the machine. It felt comfortable and safe, as though we could have done this before.

I would have liked to ride that Honda all the way to the ocean's edge, but Simon took a sharp right and steered us into the heavy traffic on the beltway and, then, several minutes later, off a ramp and onto the tree-lined George Washington Parkway into northern Virginia. Twenty minutes later we'd wound through a residential area. He zipped up the drive of an old, tiny, cracker box of a house, pulling the bike to a stop near the steps to the back porch. The door of the detached garage stood open. A baby blue 1965 Ford Mustang convertible peeked out from inside. It looked to be in mint condition.

I came off the bike, pulling off my helmet and shaking out my hair, simply glad to be out of the traffic and away from my house, away from everything I was connected with.

"You live here?" I asked.

Again, he gave me a strange look. "You know damn well I live here. What the hell's wrong with you?"

I faced him dead on. "I told you. I don't remember you."

He took a deep breath through his nose, his nostrils flaring. I could tell he wasn't pleased. I suspected he didn't believe me.

"This had better not be some game you're playing, Evie."

I roared to life. Losing my memory was bad enough. Having someone doubt it—after I'd confided in him—was intolerable.

"Believe it or don't, but don't you ever, ever call me a liar." I punched my finger right into his chest.

And he, the bastard, found that amusing. I backed away, keenly aware of how his closeness affected me.

His amusement quickly disappeared as his green eyes

boldly searched my gray ones. "You're serious."

"As serious as I've ever been in my life."

"All that at your house...You really didn't remember my name? You still don't remember me at all? Nothing?"

He seemed more hurt now than angry, and I wondered again what had happened between us. The only thing I did know was that, for some reason, I felt safe with him. If I hadn't, I never would have left my house with him, policeman or not.

"I don't remember anything after leaving home Saturday evening to meet Wes Gallagher in Dupont Circle," I confessed. "Nothing about giving you my Jeep or my keys or asking you to meet me anywhere. My memory begins again this morning sometime around one A.M."

"Let's take this inside," he said.

I could feel his frustration mirror my own as I followed him up the porch and in through the back door.

He lived in the house alone, that much was obvious. It was too small for two people. Glasses, but no plates, were stacked in the sink. I was sure if I looked in the trash there'd be plenty of fast food wrappers. No pictures hung on the walls, and only one chair was pulled up to the small breakfast table. The place was surprisingly neat. I would have suspected he was the messy type.

One of the glasses in the sink had lipstick on it. It could have been my color.

"Want something to drink?" he offered. "I need a beer. I think I've still got some Dos Equis in the fridge. Your favorite."

How did he know that? Had he bought it for me, or did we have similar tastes?

I shook my head, and he helped himself to one, studying me closely as he watched my every move. His scrutiny made me uncomfortable. Hell, being alone in the same room with the man was enough to leave me off balance.

He felt the attraction, too. I could see it in his eyes, in the way his gaze took in every curve of my body, and then came back to my eyes to challenge me to remember him. I fought to hold my breathing steady.

"That bump on your head...You were hurt," he said.

"Not badly," I assured him, keeping my distance.

"Bad enough to wipe out everything you know about me," he said.

Then I saw Simon's anger, seething inside him as his eyes narrowed and the soft line of his mouth hardened. I had no idea what had spawned it. If I'd known this man, it could only have been for a few hours, maybe a day. How could he care so much? Or did he? Maybe I was mistaking concern for something else entirely. Maybe he wanted something from me, something that had nothing whatsoever to do with the attraction between us.

"You're the one with the memory. Tell me what happened," I demanded. I understood anger, even rage, but I had no tolerance for it in anyone else. "When did I meet you? Were you with Wes when I went to see him Saturday night?"

The tenseness about his eyes relaxed just enough that I knew he'd finally accepted what I had told him. In its place was something else. Disappointment?

He took a swig of beer. "Not at first. I crashed your party."

Being with Wes was never a party. "Why?"

He hesitated. "Because I wanted to meet you. My brother was Michael Whitehall."

I felt my eyes grow wide with surprise. Michael was one of ours. He'd been the first of the August Eight to die. I'd never heard the name Simon Talbot in all my research on the families of the dead. How could Simon have slipped by me?

"I didn't know Michael had any family still living."

His father had died less than a year after the killings and his mother a year or two after that. How could I have missed the fact that Michael had a brother?

"Well, he had me," Simon said.

I immediately realized how insensitive I sounded. If Simon was telling the truth, he was one of us, every bit as much as me or Jackie or Wes.

"Michael's family was your family, too. I'm sorry."

He nodded and I could see pain in his eyes.

I wondered if Claire Williams, whose sister had died that August night and who had founded our support group, knew about Simon. Had she invited him to our group in the early days? He'd never been there. If he had, I doubted I would ever have had anything to do with Wes.

"Talbot, Whitehall," I said. "Different last names."

"Half brothers. My mother remarried when I was two. Michael came along a year later."

He seemed to be reading the skepticism in my face. I still couldn't shake the fact I'd never heard of him.

"I was working in Pennsylvania when Michael died," he said.

"As a police officer?"

He nodded. "It sort of runs in the family."

"Your stepdad."

"He was a Montgomery County cop until he died."

I could hear the pride in his voice.

I remembered his stepfather. He was assigned to the northern part of the county, but most of his hours off were spent shadowing the team working the murders that first year. I'd met him once or twice and immediately liked him.

"I'm sorry about your brother," I said.

"Yeah."

"So you weren't the reason Wes was so eager to get me to Dupont?"

"No. Whoever you were waiting for didn't show. Wes was pissed, and he wasn't particularly thrilled that I'd barged in."

"Sounds like you scared off whoever it was we were waiting for."

"Could be. You really don't remember me?"

It was more a plea than a question. His face remained passive, but the softness of his voice gave him away. There had definitely been something between us that he wanted me to remember.

As I stared into his eyes, I had one brief flash of what was almost a memory, actually more a feeling of intimacy. Then it was gone, but it left me shaken.

I shook my head. "I'm sorry."

He looked away and swore under his breath.

"I've been in this house before, haven't I?" I touched the glass in the sink, but it was more than that. The house seemed somehow familiar. I'd bet the only bathroom was upstairs, next to an unexpectedly large bedroom, but I couldn't have described any of it.

Or what had happened here.

"Yeah. You spent Saturday night here."

It was my turn to raise an eyebrow. How could I not remember that? Had I...had we...

"*All* night? What do you mean?" I asked.

"I wanted to talk to you. Privately," he added. "I invited you back here."

I could feel the heat rising in my cheeks. "Is that what we did? Talk?"

That look again, half-lidded below thick lashes, both intimate and challenging at the same time. And sexy as hell.

"Most of the time."

He drank more beer as he watched me. I could again feel the draw between us, even across the room. Had it distracted me then as much as it was distracting me now? My heart raced a little faster.

"And you don't know who I was meeting at the bar. Could it have been Isaacs?"

"Could have been anybody. All I know is by Sunday evening you weren't at all sure Isaacs had committed the August Eight murders."

I swallowed my reaction as I felt my muscles steel. I knew Luther Isaacs had killed David and Michael and the other six victims. I'd known it for fifteen years. I lifted my chin defiantly. I still knew it. Nobody could make me doubt it.

"Did I have someone else in mind?"

"No one that you shared with me."

"When did I leave here?"

"Sunday morning the phone woke us up."

Us, like a unit, not individuals sharing a house, like a couple sharing a bed.

I swallowed and forced my words to sound natural. "Who called?"

"You didn't say. It was your cell phone."

I always kept my phone on a bedside table. So we *had* been sleeping in the same room. In the same bed? Why wouldn't he just tell me?

"I don't have all the answers for you, Eva. You left this house and then came back in the evening. You asked me to keep your Jeep and to drop you back downtown. I didn't want you to go, at least not alone, but you refused to tell me who you were meeting."

"But you did let me go."

He laughed and his face softened, making him look years younger. "Let you? Have you ever tried arguing with you?"

I smiled. Maybe he did know me better than I thought. "All the time. I don't always win either. So you took me to D.C."

He nodded. "I dropped you near Dupont. You asked me to meet you near Metro Center around ten o'clock. You said if you didn't show in an hour, you'd meet me at your house. You said the house keys were on the ring with the car key, and you rattled off the security code to your system. Then you got out of the Jeep and took off across the park where I couldn't follow you—before you let me get in a question. When I tried to call your cell, you'd turned it off."

"But you still came back to get me, just as I'd asked you to."

He nodded. "I waited an hour and forty-five minutes downtown, then I went to your house in Potomac."

I must have been onto something important, and I must have thought I could handle the situation by myself. And I didn't want him to know the details. So why had I asked Simon to pick me up? Why hadn't I called Jesse or Jackie or, better yet, simply dialed 911? Why didn't I want the police involved?

Because I trusted Simon, just as my instincts were telling me to trust him now.

"How about you fill me in on this Wes dude," he said.

Was that a little bit of jealousy I detected in his voice or only contempt? Whatever it was, I could tell he had no use for Wes.

"Apparently you don't know whether or not you were with him last night, right?" he asked.

I shook my head. "I told you, I know nothing about Sunday."

"Has Wes ever harmed you or threatened to harm you?"

"No. Of course not. I've known him for years."

"He's never struck you?"

My hand went to the bump on my head. "No. Wes didn't do this."

"Are you sure? I thought you didn't remember."

"I don't. But if Wes had threatened me in any way—"

"He would have gotten the worst of it before he landed a blow." He grinned.

I blanched because he was exactly right. Is that what

had happened?

I shook off the thought, willing my heart back into a normal rhythm.

"Hey, you all right?" His posture straightened, and, for a moment, I thought he was going to come over to me. My eyes warned him to stay where he was.

"I'm fine," I assured him.

He relaxed again as he drank more of his beer, and I began to pace in front of him, his stare boring through me.

"Our focus should be on Luther Isaacs, not Wes Gallagher," I said.

"You're sure about that?"

"Yes. I was afraid as soon as Isaacs was released, he might kill again," I explained.

"And you planned to prevent that from happening."

"If I could."

Is that what I'd tried to do? I attempted to sort it out in my mind. Could Isaacs have called me to set up a meeting about my documentary? But why would he? And if he did, why would Wes be there and how had Isaacs gotten my cell phone number? I'd contacted his sister. She could have given it to him.

Had I gone off Sunday night to find or meet Isaacs and what? Kill him? I couldn't imagine doing anything like that. I hated him with ever fiber of my being, but I was no killer.

Yet there'd been blood on my hands.

Whatever I'd done, I hadn't stopped Isaacs. Instead, I'd handed him his first victim in fifteen years, Albert Haggerty. Al had a wife, a grown daughter, and two grandchildren. Count one more family destroyed. Only this time I'd had a personal hand in it.

I couldn't deal with that now. I was good at stowing away guilt, at least temporarily. I was also good at pushing down the rage that sometimes later exploded. I couldn't afford to think about Al's death right now. Isaacs wanted me dead.

And I returned the sentiment.

Had he shot at me because I'd hired Haggerty?

If Isaacs had had his way, I would have been his second victim of the night, and Simon might well have gone down with me.

"Psychopaths like Isaacs can't be rehabilitated, especially the violent ones," I rattled off as though reading from a textbook. "They don't think like you and I do. In prison they only bide time."

Of course, he'd know all about psychopaths, being a police officer.

He swallowed more beer as he leaned against the sink, taking me in. "You don't really have to be so strong, you know. Focusing on Isaacs keeps you from feeling. You can do your work without emotionally isolating yourself from the people you care about. It's all right to let yourself feel, Eva."

Anger sped up my heart. "So that's your nickel analysis of me."

"Actually, it's yours."

I felt as though I'd been slapped in the face. Exactly how intimate *had* our conversation been Saturday night? I didn't talk about my feelings with anybody.

"Is that your usual breakfast?" I asked, desperate to change the subject.

"Breakfast? I was thinking of this as a late night snack."

"After nine in the morning? When do you have to go to work?" I asked. I knew a lot of the departments in the area worked in shifts with three days off. I had no idea what the schedules were like in Pennsylvania. Or what Simon was doing with a house in northern Virginia if he worked in Pittsburgh. That would be one heck of a commute.

He shook his head and set down his beer. "I'm on indefinite leave."

"Voluntarily?" I asked.

His eyes crinkled and he offered a sarcastic grin. "At

the moment."

"How long have you had this place?"

"About a month."

Just as I thought. Simon must have come to the area because of Isaacs' release. He was on alert, as was I. All the other family members who had refused to forget and move on with their lives would be, too. If Isaacs was our devil, we were his, gathering at each of his parole hearings to make certain he stayed in prison.

But Simon had never been at any of the hearings.

Stupidly, I'd actually thought Isaacs might keep a low profile, at least for a while, giving us time to seal his fate. Instead, he'd come out guns blazing.

But why? What would Isaacs gain by killing me?

Of course. He'd stop my documentary.

"So you're after Isaacs, too," I said.

"Something like that. I'm after the person who killed my brother."

The police had had fifteen years to gather conclusive proof that Luther Isaacs had killed the August Eight, but even with someone as dedicated and capable as Jesse Sedwick at the helm, they'd never been able to do it. Neither had we.

It was Isaacs's car, all right, that the bullets had come from. I'd identified it, every detail seared into my memory. So had one other witness, but she'd died in a car accident before the trial began.

Sometimes I wished that I had identified Isaacs, too, even if I hadn't seen the shooter. But I couldn't do that. How could I honor David's memory by lying?

The police had never been able to place Isaacs behind the wheel of his car that night and that's why their case against him had fallen apart. They'd found it parked in his driveway, vacuumed and wiped clean of prints. Isaacs never wavered in his insistence that it had been stolen. The murder weapon remained unfound. The only thing that actually connected him and the car to the murders was my identification of it, and I hadn't gotten the license plate number that night.

The police had found stolen electronics in the trunk of his car with his fingerprints all over them. How high or stupid had he been to forget to also wipe the prints off the merchandise? The theft had bought Isaacs a fifteen-year prison sentence with the possibility of parole after five. The combination of Isaacs' refusal to admit his guilt for the theft, and the public outrage that would have erupted if he'd been released, meant he'd never made parole. He'd served every day of his sentence. Fifteen years wasn't enough. Maybe for theft, but certainly not for murder.

"We've got to get him," I stated.

"Before he gets us?" Simon suggested.

"That would be good," I agreed.

If it had been simple, we would have done it years ago. But we were all handicapped. We'd all dealt with our losses in different ways. Simon had become a police officer, Claire Williams a grief counselor, and Jackie had married a rich man almost old enough to be her father and spent his money. Wes never grew up. Me? I was a paranoid woman with relationship issues who made documentaries about psychopaths. The others—well, they would all tell me how they'd dealt or not dealt over the years as I put our story on film.

"Where do we start?" I asked.

"In here." He motioned toward his living room, and I followed him in. He had the confident movements of a man who was used to being in charge. I liked that—except when it interfered with me giving the orders. Any relationship between us would be potentially explosive.

He turned and watched me walk past him, waiting for a glimmer of recognition.

What I saw made me stop still.

Chapter 4

The room was not more than a twelve-by-twelve box with worn hardwood floors and dingy paint that had once been white. The only furniture was a desk, a chair, and a large filing cabinet. But I hardly noticed the furniture. All four walls were papered with notes written in heavy black marker. Photos of each of the eight victims were surrounded by information: when and where they died, family histories, resumes, a timeline of what each of them had been doing the night they died. I was stunned.

The enormity of what we'd lost that August night overwhelmed me again. I could feel the tears rising in my eyes. I tried to will them away. It'd been a long time since I'd cried over that night.

Immediately to my right was Edwina Jackson's picture. She had been 76 years old, African-American, a grandmother of six, and the heart of her large family. Artistic, she'd worked part-time arranging flowers for a florist. She died while sweeping the sidewalk in front of her house. Three of her grandchildren were inside watching TV.

Next to her was Dennis Toro, an immigrant from the Philippines. He was the father of six children and ran a magazine kiosk at a Rockville mall. He'd just gotten off from work and was mowing his lawn.

On the opposite wall was Karen Durwood, 51, mother and civil engineer working with the Department of Defense. She'd been setting out the trash for the next day's pickup. Within months her husband had been hospitalized with depression. He grieved himself to death two years later. Her son had needed more help than Claire's support group could provide, essentially having lost both his parents that night in August. He was a loner and he was trouble.

I touched Sabrina Tyler's photo. So young, so vibrant. Wes said he'd planned to marry her. I wondered if he'd ever told her or if he'd developed the fantasy after her death. She was a beautiful creature, slim, darkly exotic, with blue eyes that looked almost black in this photo. She'd stepped outside the dance for a cigarette. She never came back in.

Her death had shattered Wes, leaving him an irresponsible charmer with a childish temper and commitment issues even bigger than mine.

On the same wall was Horace Gonzalez, 44, frozen in time, a saucy, flirtatious smile staring back at me. He was a brick layer who loved salsa dancing, and he was Jackie's father. She and I had met through Claire's group. We understood each other, how one moment can change your life forever. She never questioned my moods or, except for Wes, the men I was involved with. And I never criticized the shoes she bought.

I turned. Across the room was April Bennett, registered nurse, 31, and Claire Williams' twin. Her husband had remarried within nine months. When I'd called to speak with him about the documentary, he wouldn't talk to me on the phone. She'd left behind twin six-year-old girls. One was now in her last year of college on a full academic scholarship. The other was a high school drop out and the source of much of Claire's angst.

Claire's group and her friendship had saved my sanity. We'd all had our lives altered fifteen years ago, but it had affected us in different ways. I'd formed a bond with them all, all the families and friends who'd lost people that night, regardless of their abilities to cope. An even stronger bond than I had with my own parents. All they'd wanted was for me to be all right again, to be the girl I'd been before. She was gone for good. She'd died with David. The other survivors understood that, but none of the others had witnessed the shootings.

The downside to all the grief we'd shared was my knowing what it was like to lose a mother, a father, a sibling, a lover. This room represented all of that loss, all of that emotion. Life was incredibly fragile. Claire had never meant for any of us to take all of that on, certainly not me. Unforeseen consequences of very good intentions.

Claire. She brought me comfort and offered me unconditional love. But she didn't understand anything about me. She blamed the breakup of my marriages on my inability to move on. I blamed them on my unhealthy interest in reckless men and loved her anyway.

I turned away from David's photo. He'd been tall, broad-shouldered, and blond. But the only memory I could summon now was how he looked as he lay dying in my arms.

I pushed the image from my mind and turned toward Simon, who was very much alive. His wall could add nothing to what I knew about David and that night. Or what his family had been through. And what I'd been through. I'd had blood on my hands that night, too.

"What I don't understand is why Isaacs would expose himself by killing Haggerty and shooting at me," I said, clearing my throat and forcing myself to focus on what had happened early this morning. "The police were never able to link the bullets at the homicides or any weapons, for that matter, to Isaacs."

"Who says he exposed himself? Whoever shot at us used a shotgun," Simon pointed out. "Shot can't be traced. It doesn't produce barrel markings like other guns. If Isaacs is behind it like you think he is, maybe Haggerty's death was simply a warning to you to back off. 'Don't put a tail on me.'"

"Could be." If so, what an incredible waste. A human life reduced to a threat.

"Haggerty wasn't killed with a shotgun," I stated,

focusing on the facts. It was the only way I could keep my composure.

"No. I'm guessing a .45," Simon agreed.

"Why switch guns?"

"Maybe he was shot at close range."

In another location. With a silencer. If Al had been killed downtown, Isaacs would have been crazy to use a shotgun.

I wondered if the bullet was still in the body or if it had gone straight through. Isaacs may have dug it out before dumping the body. Even high, as he'd been that night fifteen years ago, Isaacs was sufficiently aware of what he was doing to dispose of any evidence of the murders. My bet was he'd also covered the soles of his shoes and worn gloves when he dumped Haggerty's body—and when he'd shot at me. He would have left no prints, no DNA, only the body and the destruction to my house. He'd had fifteen years to plan what he would do once he was free, fifteen years of accumulating anger.

He wanted me dead because I wouldn't let the August Eight be forgotten. Because I'd hired a private detective to document his every move. Because he knew how much I hated him. Because he knew my documentary was intended to send him straight back to jail.

I noticed one cluster had a wall of its own. I moved closer. Michael Whitehall. Simon's half-brother. He'd lingered for a week with a bullet wound to his head, the only one of the eight to survive more than minutes. Then he'd died, like all the rest. He'd been cremated. There'd been no public ceremony.

He'd shown great promise as a cop. A couple of weeks before his death, he'd foiled an attempt on a witness's life during a transfer from a safe house to the courthouse. He was being hailed a hero only to be gunned down himself.

I studied the photo, Michael's senior picture for his

high school yearbook, as Simon watched me closely.

"I know you were proud of him. The two of you don't look much alike." Of course fifteen years of grief altered anyone, both inside and out. The hard lines on Simon's lean face had nothing to do with the youthful roundness of eighteen-year-old Michael.

"So people told us."

I dropped my gaze and turned back toward him. It seemed somehow obscene to be reading about his brother's death with him standing right there.

"Did you find a pattern?" I asked. I was again in control. Focusing on the facts, rather than the victims, was the only way I could keep my thinking straight.

He shook his head. "Outside of the time frame and the geography, there was no pattern."

"It was a thrill kill spree," I agreed, "relying only on opportunity. Contrary to public opinion, most psychopaths don't need patterns."

And psychopaths had no trouble lying. That was the one hitch with Isaacs and the only thing about him that gave me pause. He refused to admit his guilt, or show remorse. Why would he do that when it meant he would serve every day of his fifteen-year sentence? Arrogance? The need to feel superior? Quite possibly. Now Isaacs was free—without parole—and no one had any idea where he was.

"It was a spree," I repeated. "Nothing more."

Nothing more to Isaacs. So very much more to those of us left behind.

"You're sure Isaacs did it." Simon watched for my reaction.

"Yes. He might have been hopped up on drugs and not remember doing it, but he did."

"You should let the police take care of Isaacs."

"Is that what you intend to do?" I asked.

"Of course."

Then why was he here? Or was Simon referring to himself rather than the Montgomery County Police Department?

"The police had their fifteen years. It's my turn now," I said.

"Suit yourself," was all he said, but I could tell that wasn't what he was thinking.

"Just say it."

"You've done some incredible documentary work in the past. You're single-minded, pretty much unstoppable once you take on a project. Hell, you even amassed enough evidence to get two convictions."

So he'd followed my work. "Wow. I had no idea you were such a fan."

"But..."

"But what?"

"You're too close to this one," he warned.

I stared a hole through his attractive face. I'd heard it all before, from Wes, from Jackie, from Jesse, even from my producer. I was making my documentary. I was going to bury Isaacs. They — including Simon — could all get used to it.

"You know someone better qualified?"

He shook his head. "But why now, Eva? You've got to know you're baiting Isaacs."

"Documentaries cost lots of money to make. Isaacs' pending release generated enough interest in the press this summer that I was finally able to get enough backing for the project. I would have done it ten years ago if I could have made anyone care."

The public was fickle. How attached could they get to the victims of one tragedy when there was a fresh one each morning on the news?

"Isaacs has been convicted by the media," he said.

"That's right. I'll take a victory wherever I can get it. Now what we need is the kind of conviction that counts."

I was finished with this subject. I felt no need to defend myself to anyone, not even to Simon.

"Got any food in this place?" I asked. Not only had I not slept in at least twenty-four hours, I had no idea when I'd had my last meal.

"Nothing I'd feed you. But there's a pancake house around the corner. Are you up for that? They've got real maple syrup."

"Sure."

I didn't have much of an appetite, but if I'd let the murders affect my eating habits, I would have been dead from starvation years ago. I needed my strength. I intended to live to see Isaacs get what he deserved.

Eggs Benedict proved not to be the best choice considering how empty my stomach was, but I wolfed it down. Simon had a Belgian waffle, bacon and sausage. Maybe that was the problem. I kept thinking about all that syrup and butter on top of that beer he'd had.

Or maybe it was watching my very attractive companion and not knowing what exactly it was that had happened between us. I had a vivid enough imagination that I was pretty sure it was one memory I didn't want to lose.

My cell phone rang. It was Jesse, no doubt wanting to know where I was. I was irritated with the intrusion, and I had no intention of answering his questions. I couldn't tolerate too much fatherly concern right now, and I knew he wouldn't approve of my staying with Simon. For Jesse, I was still seventeen years old. I didn't answer. Instead, I turned off my phone, and tried to finish the little that was left on my plate.

By the time we walked back to Simon's house, exhaustion had hit us both hard. We agreed on a nap. Two hours, three at the most. By noon we'd be up. I had an appointment later that afternoon I needed to keep. In the evening I'd go by the bar in Dupont where I'd met Wes and talk to the bartender. I'd been there Saturday evening, maybe Sunday as well. He might remember seeing me.

"You can sleep in my bed," Simon offered.

His offer brought me up short. What was he suggesting?

"I couldn't put you on the couch," I insisted.

"I didn't intend for you to."

Again, he gave me that half-lidded look and I blushed. I knew he was every bit as attracted to me as I was to him.

"It's a queen bed," he said quickly. "We're both tired. I assure you I won't bother you."

He bothered me just by standing next to me, even as tired as I was.

"I'll take the couch." If he wouldn't tell me what happened, I wasn't about to share his bed.

"Suit yourself, but I warn you, the previous tenants left it here, and they had a dog."

It was in a narrow room off the kitchen. Between the lumps on the sofa, the strong doggy odor, and the Hollandaise sauce, it promised to be an interesting couple of hours.

The breeze lifts my hair and pulls at the skirt of my white sundress, as David grabs my hand. He pulls me along with a laugh as though I hadn't said a word to him, my heels clinking against the sidewalk cement.

"We need to talk this out," I insist.

"No, we don't," he teases. "I already know what you're going to say." He tucks my hand into the crook of his elbow. "Besides, we can talk anytime. When are we going to have another beautiful evening like this?"

I try to pull my hand free, but he holds onto it. It is a perfect day, not too warm and quiet. There's almost no traffic. Everyone must be at the beach or having barbecues.

"David, please."

A beat-up blue Ford Fairmont with a gray patch on the fender creeps up our street. It's driving too slowly. I stop and stare. Something about it...

"Eva, what's wrong?" David asks.

I don't answer. I just watch as the car creeps closer. It has a pine tree air freshener swinging from the rear view mirror.

As it draws alongside of us, a shadow of a hand gripping something appears near the passenger window as the driver leans over. My mouth opens in a scream, as David steps in front of me. Fire spews from the barrel. And David turns to me, a look of surprise on his face. My white sundress is splattered with red. I watch as David sinks to the ground. Then I'm on the ground, too, cradling David in my arms, his blood soaking through my clothes and pooling on the sidewalk beneath us. I again open my mouth to scream, but I can't breathe I can't breathe I —

I jerked straight up on the couch, gasping, sweat drenching my body, my heart racing. I'd dreamed of David's death for fifteen years, but now it was as though I was living it all again. What had happened Sunday? If Wes was all right, surely he would have returned my calls. Not knowing was far worse than knowing no matter how bad it was, unless...unless I'd caused something to happen that was so terrible my mind refused to let me remember it.

I shook off the thought. It was David's death that I'd witnessed in that drive-by shooting. Surely if I'd seen someone else die, I'd be dreaming about that instead of David. I'd learned not to let my dreams rule my life. They were dreams, nothing else, I insisted to myself. They solved nothing.

I took a couple of deep breaths and looked at my watch. It was almost noon. The smell of coffee was coming from the kitchen. Simon must be up, too. I found him in the living room, brooding in his desk chair, his legs crossed, staring at the walls. He didn't even turn around when I came in.

I walked closer and laid my hand on his shoulder. I could feel the tension in his muscles. I knew too well the frustration he was feeling and the need to somehow ease it.

"If there is some clue on these walls," I said quietly, "he left us too many directions to look in. We need to look forward. My bet is Isaacs made contact with his sister in Fredericksburg, Virginia."

Simon turned and looked up at me, as he covered my hand with his own, sending sparks up my arm. "Did you ever interview her?"

I shook my head, reclaiming my hand and moving several feet away. His gesture was too familiar for me to be comfortable with, especially when it left me so off balance.

"She wouldn't speak with me, other than to call me a few choice names. She believes Isaacs is innocent."

Add Isaacs' own family to the list of those he'd destroyed.

"Help yourself to some coffee," Simon offered.

I poured a cup of the thick liquid in the kitchen and turned on the small TV sitting on the counter. The coffee had been sitting for some time. He'd made it strong. Now it was more like sludge. It made me wonder if Simon had lain down at all.

I flipped through the channels to one that had the noon news already in progress. A story about Haggerty's death and the shooting at my home was wrapping up. It seemed surreal to watch a news woman with a microphone broadcasting live from my front yard.

The news continued with no mention of anyone being injured or killed anywhere near Dupont. Whatever had happened, at least I hadn't left a body behind. I was about to flip it off when the newscaster repeated the top story.

"Approximately one hour ago, Claire Williams, a well known area psychologist, was shot at her clinic in Bethesda. She's been transported to Baptist Hospital. Police are speculating she might be the victim of the same individual who shot into the home of documentary film maker Eva Keller over night. Both women have connections to the August Eight murders that took place in Montgomery County fifteen years ago."

A picture of Isaacs filled the screen with a telephone number across the bottom.

"If anyone has seen Luther Isaacs," the announcer continued, "immediately contact the Montgomery County Police Department."

I stared at the screen, blinking back tears and refusing to believe what I was hearing. Not Claire. Dear God. She had a husband and children. She couldn't die. They needed her. *I* needed her.

Simon came up behind me and touched my arms. I jumped.

"You all right?"

I was shaking so hard I had to steady myself against the counter.

"You're white as a ghost." He turned off the TV and tipped my chin upward so he could get a better look at my face. "What's wrong?"

"Isaacs shot Claire."

Simon's face darkened into anger. "How bad is she? Did they say?"

I shook my head, tears clogging my throat.

Simon pulled me into his arms, cradling me against his chest, and I let him, as the tears spilled freely.

"Shhhh," he soothed. "It's going to be all right."

"You don't know that," I said angrily and attempted to push him away. But he held me fast. My tears involuntarily turned to sobs, and I allowed him to comfort me.

"She can't die. I can't lose Claire," I whispered, clutching Simon. "He can't do this to me again."

Claire was almost like a mother to me, and I loved her

dearly. She and Jackie were my family. Much of my strength and certainly my bravado came only because I knew she was always behind me, loving me, understanding so much about me, even when she didn't approve of what I did.

"I know what she means to you."

I pulled back enough to look into Simon's eyes.

"You told me about her Saturday night when you saw the photo of her sister on the wall." He drew me back against his chest, smoothing my hair. "If she were critical, they would have said so. She'll be all right."

I broke free and took a step back, swiping the tears from my eyes. "I have to go see her."

"Of course. Did they say when this happened?"

"Sometime while I was sleeping."

He nodded, his face grim. "You do realize this shooting might be an attempt to bring you to the hospital."

I looked at him as though he'd grown two heads. "What are you talking about?"

"Could be Isaacs or whoever is doing this wants you and the other family members who kept him in prison dead, and he's planning to pick you off one by one. But it could also be that he wants to draw you out of hiding. It could be a trap."

"At the hospital?"

"Wherever he can get you to show up. You may be the primary target."

Simon had already pulled a shoulder holster out of one of the kitchen drawers and was fastening it around him. He extracted a .44 Magnum from the same drawer, shoved a loaded clip into it, and holstered the gun. Then he slipped on a jacket. I could have kissed him. I'd been prepared for a fight, but he wasn't even going to try to talk me out of going.

"You good with your revolver?" he asked.

"I am." I was completely composed now. Adrenaline had dried my tears and kicked me into action.

"Good. Did they say which hospital Claire is in?"

"Baptist."

I watched the man, amazed that he seemed to respect me enough not to make it more difficult for me. I was used to criticism.

"Thanks," I said.

"For what?"

I shook my head and he didn't press it.

"They may have a guard on her door, but I'll show them my badge. I think they'll let us see her."

"Assuming she can even talk," I said more to myself than to Simon.

I transferred a handful of bullets from my jacket into my jeans pocket, stuffed my gun snugly back into the loop sewn into the back of my jeans, and headed for the door.

Isaacs had better not have hurt Claire too badly, the bastard. Shooting at me was one thing, but he was not going to get away with hurting her. If his fight was with me, I'd be ready for him.

Chapter 5

Jesse Sedwick was standing just inside the door when we got to Claire's room at the hospital. He looked every one of his fifty-seven years, with his blue shirt unbuttoned at his neck, his tie loosened at his throat, and a plaid sport coat from sometime during the last decade. He was still fit, even though he'd been retired for almost two years. Most of his brown hair had gone gray, including his mustache. His face was drawn, and I knew the shootings must have stirred up the same emotions in him that they had in me.

As soon as he saw us, he stepped into the hallway and pulled me into a hug, whispering in my ear how much he'd been worried about me. I almost lost it as I had with Simon, but I managed to tamp down my fear of losing Claire and of once again being part of a string of precious lives taken. It was tempting to give it all over to Jesse, to collapse against him and become the child who needed protection. That's what Jesse wanted me to do, but I wasn't seventeen anymore. I was a grown woman, and I had a job to do. If Jesse had his way, he wouldn't let me do it. He'd never look at me like an equal the way Simon did. I pulled out of his grip.

"Is Claire going to be all right?" I asked him, as I forced myself to look into her room through the open door. She was lying so still in the bed. Bandages covered one shoulder and both her forearms. Her porcelain skin was even paler than usual, and her short, light blonde hair lay limp against her head. I hardly breathed until I saw her eyes flutter. Her husband Bill and a nurse were both bending over her. She seemed unaware that Simon and I were waiting in the hallway.

Jesse nodded. "She'll be fine. She has a couple of deep cuts and some bruises, but none of her injuries are anything to be concerned about. The doctors didn't have much more to do than a clean and patch job."

"But she was shot," I insisted.

"Actually, no. The media is making more out of this than it is. Her injuries are from a few bits of glass that flew out where the shot came through the window of her office. Apparently she moved out of the direct line of fire before the bullet hit."

"Then why are they keeping her in the hospital?"

"She's having some arrhythmia, so they want to watch her overnight."

I was amazed she wasn't dead. Had Isaacs' aim or his reflexes deteriorated that much while he was in prison? He'd seemed right on when he'd shot at me.

"The window didn't shatter?" Simon asked.

"It was triple ply insulated something or other. It seems to have held pretty well, except for where the bullets came through. And you are..."

"Jesse Sedwick meet Simon Talbot," I said, stepping between them. I didn't need Jesse assessing my companions. "Simon's—"

"Nice to meet you," Simon said, cutting me off and offering Jesse his hand.

Jesse's gaze darted back and forth between us.

"You should come stay with Nina and me until the police pick up Isaacs," Jesse offered. "Nina's been after me to get hold of you and bring you home with me. She's even put clean sheets on the guest bed."

"Nina's a sweetheart but the two of you don't need to worry about me, Jesse. I can take care of myself."

"Is that what you were doing this morning when that maniac took a shot at you?" he asked.

And with that we were officially back to our usual

roles: child and overprotective parent. I shrugged him off, irritated as hell. A lot of years had passed since Jesse had played surrogate father to me. I didn't intend to let him slip back into that role. Besides, I'd come to see Claire, not Jesse.

"Give Nina my love," I said, as I brushed past him and stuck my head through the doorway. Simon stayed behind with Jesse in the hallway.

I caught Claire's eye and she offered me a shadow of that colossal smile of hers.

"Eva." Her voice sighed with relief. "They told me you were shot at, too." Her gaze traced the scratches on my cheek and neck and settled on the bump on my forehead. "Have you let a doctor look at you?"

"I'm fine. Really," I insisted as I came to her bedside. She took my hand. "*You're* the one in the hospital bed. What happened?"

"I feel like a fool." She rolled her eyes, trying to make light of her situation. That was Claire's way. Death didn't scare her either. She didn't welcome it, but she didn't resent it the way that I did.

"You know the large room in the back where I hold my group counseling sessions?"

I nodded. "It backs up onto a stand of greenery."

"Right. I went in there to set up for my ten-thirty group session, opened the blinds, and something flew through the glass. You would think with Isaacs' release I'd have the sense not to open the idiotic blinds. I could have just turned on the lights."

I squeezed her hand. "So you didn't see anything."

"Nothing." Her expression turned sober. "Eva, you need to get yourself out of here to someplace safe. And the others..."

"Trust me, Claire, dying's not at the top of my list of things to do." I leaned in and kissed her cheek. She winced and I realized she was in more pain than she wanted to let on.

She'd probably had a bad fall to the floor.

"I called Jackie on the way over here and told her to warn the others," I said.

"Good. If any of the phone numbers she has are out of date, she can get a list from my secretary. And—"

"Shhhh," I soothed. "The only person you need to be worrying about right now is yourself. We can take care of ourselves."

"Have you talked to Wes?" she asked.

I shook my head. She didn't need to know that he wasn't returning my calls.

"He won't listen to Jackie. He may even panic. If you can't get through to him, have Jesse call him."

I nodded. She was right. Wes had had a troubled childhood even before the August Eight shootings, winding up in juvenile hall more than once. Jesse had become something of a mentor to him even before the shootings. He was the one person who could usually get through to Wes.

I said good-bye to Claire and then to Jesse in the hallway, telling him what Claire had said. He was still insistent that I come home with him, but I refused, agreeing to call him later.

As Simon and I left, Bill brushed past us on his way to the coffee machine. I grabbed his elbow and whispered in his ear. "When Claire's well enough to leave the hospital, take her and your kids someplace nobody knows about. And don't let her talk you out of it."

He pulled back and looked into my eyes, his face ashen. Then he nodded.

As I punched the elevator button, I was swamped with guilt. If I could have remembered what had happened Sunday night, would Claire be lying in that hospital bed right now? Had Wes been Isaacs' first victim after his release? Had I witnessed his death? Had it frightened me so much that I'd blocked out what I'd seen?

Or had I been the one to harm someone? The thought made blood pound in my ears. I *had* to have answers. I had to know whose blood had been on my hands before someone else got hurt.

As the elevator doors closed, Simon turned to face me.

"What claim does Jesse have on you?" he asked.

I could tell from his expression, Simon didn't like Det. Jesse Sedwick one bit.

"None, really. He investigated the August Eight case. And he was especially concerned with how the deaths affected the youngest of us, but that's it."

"You might want to tell him that."

I considered Simon's words. I'm not surprised they didn't like one another. Jesse liked being in charge. And my guess was Simon didn't take well to orders, although I suspected he did fine with his superior officers.

"Gave you the third degree, did he?"

"He tried."

"What'd you tell him?"

"Everything that was any of his business."

"Right."

Jesse was hard on Wes as well and every other man that had ever come into my life. He meant well, but he couldn't be responsible for the entire world. I'd grown up a lot during the last fifteen years, and I really didn't need someone hovering over me passing judgment on my every action. Or my every suitor.

Simon's baby blue Mustang was waiting for us in the hospital parking lot. We both took a quick look around. If anyone was waiting for us, we couldn't make them.

As I climbed into the passenger seat and Simon slid beneath the wheel, my cell phone beeped. I'd missed a call. Finally. Wes.

I flipped on my phone. But it hadn't been Wes. It was from a number I wasn't familiar with. As I held it, the phone rang, the same number registering as the one I'd missed. I answered it.

"Yes," I said.

"Eva Keller?"

"Yes," I repeated.

"This is Mary Ann Strohmeyer. I've spoken with you before. I'm Luther Isaacs' sister."

The woman I had no sympathy for—the woman who wouldn't return my calls or answer any of my letters—wanted to talk to me. Why?

I caught Simon's eye and held the phone between us so he could hear what she was saying. I held my voice steady as I answered her. "What do you want?"

"The police are looking for Luther. He didn't do it." Her voice was thin and pleading. It was obvious she'd been crying for some time. "You have to tell them he didn't shoot Claire, Eva. You know he wouldn't do that."

"No, I don't know that."

She paused. "Of course you do. Please, Eva, can you meet me?"

Simon nodded.

"What for?"

"I have something to give to you, something that will help prove Luther's innocence."

Whatever she had, it wouldn't do that.

"Where is your brother?" I asked, wondering even as I said the words why I'd bothered to ask. I wouldn't believe anything she said.

"I don't know. But he was with me until last night."

So she wasn't trying to offer him an alibi. That surprised me.

"He didn't shoot Claire," she repeated. "He couldn't have. All he wants is this nightmare to be over."

I paused, wondering why I hadn't hung up on her.

"If this is a setup—"

"No. I swear it's not. I swear on my children's lives."

She had two children: a boy seven, and a girl ten. But could I believe her? I doubted she was a good enough actress to fake the choking I could hear over the phone.

"One hour," I said. "Blue line. Smithsonian Metro station. Get there by Metro. Step out of the car and wait for me on the platform."

Again, Simon nodded his approval.

With the security around the D.C. Metro stations, I wondered if she'd dare bring a weapon down there. Then I realized what an irrational thought that was. My nerves were really on edge. I couldn't really imagine Mary Ann, a mother of two, attacking me in a public place. Her brother, however, was another matter.

"How will I find you?" she asked.

"You won't," I told her. "I'll find you."

I ended the call.

I had no use for Mary Ann Isaacs Strohmeyer. Intellectually, I knew she was probably as much a victim as the rest of us because of her brother's actions fifteen years ago, yet a part of me irrationally viewed her as an accomplice. Maybe it was because she so steadfastly denied his guilt. Maybe it was because she and her brother had the same eyes. Maybe it was because I'd long ago lost all objectivity.

In any case, I was not anxious to see her. My head, however, told me not to pass up any opportunities. In trying to prove his innocence, his sister might just help me convict her brother.

"Wait for me here," I insisted to Simon at the top of the escalators that descended deep into the Metro system.

"No way am I letting you go down there alone," Simon retorted.

I could tell by the set of his jaw I'd have to chain him to the bicycle racks to keep him from coming with me — and even then I wasn't sure that would work.

"She's one woman—" I began.

"You have no reason to believe Mary Ann will come alone," he pointed out. "Someone might come in her place. Or someone might follow her."

Sheesh! Simon was even more paranoid than I was, assuming that were possible.

"One quick shove onto the live rail of the tracks and you'd fry instantly," he went on.

"Okay, okay, already. But leave the imagery up here. I'll be careful, and you'll be my backup. I want a good twenty feet between the two of us, not a foot closer. Agreed?"

Simon gave a quick nod. He was armed, as was I, even though guns were illegal in the District. Despite all of the upgraded security, including armed guards, they had yet to put metal detectors in the Metro.

"Good. Just keep me in sight, and I'll let you know if I need you."

I stepped onto the moving steps and Simon waited, letting a dozen or so tourists crowd in between us before he joined the flow. In truth, it made me feel better to know that he'd be close by watching, just in case Isaacs and Mary Ann did have some kind of crazy trap in mind.

I went through one of the turnstiles and made it down another escalator. I spotted Mary Ann right away. She was pacing at the other end of the platform, apparently expecting me to come in on one of the trains.

She was wearing a long, all weather coat and little, if any, makeup on her anxious face. Her blonde hair was barely combed. The cut of her clothes and her shoes told me she usually took more care with her appearance.

She held tight to a briefcase that made me more than a little nervous. She must have had her coat on when she called me. She lived south, in Virginia. I'd barely given her time to get there.

She glanced behind her and spotted me right away. Her expression turned almost to relief and then back to fear when she saw my face. I hid fear fairly well, but not anger. I came up next to her, hoping not to attract the attention of the guard who was standing several yards away.

"Lose the look," I whispered to her. "Give me a quick hug. Old friends meeting," I coached.

She forced a smile and gave me a tentative hug, whispering in my ear, "Thank you for coming."

We sat down on a bench. There were several minutes between cars. Rush hour would not begin for another couple of hours.

"You know Luther isn't capable of shooting either you or Claire."

"I don't know that."

She seemed surprised by the harshness in my voice. She might have forgiven her brother for what he'd done, but I hadn't.

"He doesn't even have a weapon, and I don't keep any in the house."

I didn't bother to point out to her how naive her statement was. If thugs could buy guns out of the trunks of cars on D.C. streets, Isaacs easily could have armed himself.

"Exactly when did you last see him?" I asked.

She hesitated a moment too long. "Late yesterday evening.

"I brought this for you," she said offering the briefcase. "It's all the letters Luther wrote to me while he was in prison. He spent all those years trying to sort out what happened that night. I want you to read them."

I glanced quickly behind me. Simon was on the other side of the platform, standing as though he were waiting for a train going in the opposite direction.

"Open it," I ordered.

"Here? Why?"

"If there's a bomb inside, you're going down with me."

Her face bristled with indignation and something akin to incomprehension. "I have children. Do you really think—"

"Open it," I repeated. I wasn't about to get into a discussion over what I believed. Caution could never be sacrificed to prevent hurt feelings, not in my world.

She undid the clasps and raised the lid. She lifted the stacks of letters that filled every inch of space, sifting through them to show me that nothing else was inside, then shut the lid and clasped it back.

"Satisfied?"

"Perfectly."

"Read them. Please. Use them in your documentary. I didn't always think he was innocent either. He was a good kid. I know he made mistakes, but not the ones you seem to think he did."

A train pulled into the station and she stood up.

"He was framed fifteen years ago. You can't let it happen again. You owe him that much."

I was surprised she had the audacity to say that to me.

"I *owe* him nothing. He owes me and a lot of other people the last fifteen years of our lives."

I grabbed her wrist as she turned to leave.

"Where is he?" I asked again.

"I don't know."

"If you're harboring him, I'll see to it that you're prosecuted," I promised.

"He's only wanted for questioning," she said evenly. She stared into my eyes and I could see genuine anger.

"For now," I assured her. I let go of her and watched her walk away. She might think that Isaacs' letters would exonerate him, but I didn't. As slanted as they were sure to be, someplace in them he might have left some incriminating statement. If nothing else, they'd give me an idea of how his mind worked. I'd use anything anyone gave me to get him.

And I would get him. The question was whether or not I'd be able to do it before he killed again.

Chapter 6

I threw the briefcase Mary Ann had given me into the backseat of the '65 Mustang convertible. It was too cold to be riding around with the top down but it was the one part of the car Simon had yet to restore.

"What's in the bag she gave you?" Simon asked, as I climbed into the front seat beside him.

"Reading material. According to Mary Ann, Luther Isaacs' handwritten letters will absolutely convince me of his innocence."

"You plan to use them to convict him."

"I'm not sure if you can read my mind or if we simply think alike."

"No, Eva, we don't think alike."

I stared at his handsome profile, wondering what he meant by that comment. Without another word, Simon put the car in gear and pulled into traffic. And I was reminded, once more, that I knew next to nothing about Simon Talbot.

The tourists were out and the streets were clogged with both pedestrians and cars. But then the streets were always clogged in D.C. Driving here evoked an interesting mixture of patience, aggression, and prayer.

"Where to?" Simon asked, his voice again warm and friendly as though our previous exchange had never happened.

"Straight up 16th to Silver Spring. Haggerty's office."

"But he's dead."

"His wife will be there, going through everything he had on Isaacs."

"Not mourning? Not planning his funeral?"

"Nope. Wilma suffered from empty nest syndrome for about two years before throwing her lot in with Al. She's almost as good as he was. They've both had their funerals planned and paid for for years. If one died on the job, the other was to get whoever was responsible."

"Sounds like a nice family."

"They were. You would have liked Al. But you're going to love Wilma."

Just as I suspected. Wilma was literally in the middle of her work when we got to the offices of Haggerty & Haggerty, Private Investigations. All sixty years and two-hundred pounds of her on her five-foot, three-inch frame were surrounded by papers and photos as she sat on the hardwood floor. The place was a small, storefront walk-up in a cluster of office buildings behind a shopping center.

She looked up when she heard us come through the door, a gun in her hand. When she saw it was me, she laid the weapon back down on the floor next to her. For half a moment, I could see the determination in her eyes flicker as grief shone through. Then it was replaced by frustration.

"Anything?" I asked with no introductions, no civilities.

She shook her head. "The last I heard from Al was Sunday evening. He was downtown, heading in the direction of Dupont Circle, Isaacs in his sights."

"What time?"

"I'd say around nine. I can check the phone."

"That's close enough."

Simon and I exchanged looks. So I could have met with Isaacs. And Al would have been close by. If I'd been in any danger, he would have stepped in.

Is that how he'd died? Trying to protect me? Was it his blood I'd had on my hands? I closed my eyes and shuddered at the thought.

I'd known Al for years. He'd worked on some of the cases I'd documented. That's how I'd met him. He wouldn't let me use him on camera for obvious reasons, but he was always willing to steer me in the right direction off record. He'd proved to be an invaluable resource. He had a fascination with psychopaths just like I did.

"You all right?" Simon asked, touching my arm.

"I'm fine," I assured him.

"Who's the eye candy?" Wilma asked, nodding at Simon as though he couldn't hear her.

I laughed out loud. Part of Wilma's training had been reading forties hard boiled private eye fiction. At least she'd updated the vernacular.

"Simon Talbot, Pittsburgh P.D.," he said, offering her his hand along with his smile.

"Don't say." She stretched her hand toward him for a brief shake, then took a good look at him up and down. "You're a bit out of your territory."

"Simon is Michael Whitehall's brother," I explained.

She didn't question it, most likely out of respect for me, but she couldn't entirely hide the surprise in her eyes.

"So you're helping Eva out. You two make a good team?"

"We're heading in that direction," he assured her, his smile still teasing the corner of his mouth. Simon was obviously enjoying Wilma.

"Just checking. It's important, you know. Compatibility. It has to be all the way around."

Whatever inference Wilma was making I'd just as soon she didn't. Thinking about Simon as a partner, in more ways than one, was entirely too distracting.

"Take me and my Al," Wilma continued. "He wasn't much to look at now but you should have seen him in his younger days. My, oh, my. That man could send sparks through me with just a glance. But when you've been married as long as we were, all you see is what's inside."

Al was a good guy. Wilma would miss him like crazy. So would I.

"I'm sorry." I had to say it although I knew she wouldn't want me to.

"Yeah. Me, too," she said, biting her lip. "But it wasn't your fault, and I won't have you thinking it was. Al knew exactly what he was dealing with. All it takes is one second of letting your guard down." She offered a brave smile. "Besides, sometimes dying's part of the business. Hell, I'm amazed he lasted as long as he did."

It was all for show. Once she stopped running so fast trying to figure out who killed Al, she'd fall apart. I knew it. She knew it. But neither of us dared to acknowledge it. Not until we'd gotten the bastard.

"You've got yourself a good gal here," she told Simon. "She's smart and she's tough. But don't let her fool you. She's like a roasted marshmallow: charred and a little bitter on the outside, but all sweet goo on the inside."

"I was beginning to suspect as much," Simon agreed.

"Hey!" I interjected. "I'm in the room. And my core is pure steel."

That cracked them both up.

Nothing like a little disrespect to put one in one's place. I was feeling severely outnumbered and ready to be gone. "I need Al's reports."

Wilma gathered together what she had and pushed herself upright, holding the stack toward me, her face again serious, her hand shaking slightly. "This belongs to you. I've already gone through it and made copies of my own."

I took the papers and photos. "Thanks."

"I'll be working this end," she assured me. "I should have Al's car no later than tomorrow. They've got it in the impound."

"The police are going to release it to you that quickly?"

I asked.

"Not the police, the guys in charge of the lot. They have no idea that car might have any relevance to a murder. All I have to do is pay the ticket and the tow charge. It was picked up this morning for being parked too long in a two-hour zone."

Simon beat me to the question. "Where?"

"Near Dupont."

So Al hadn't made it out of D.C.

But his body had.

"The police will be all over it," I insisted.

"Not until I give it back to them." Her face was set.

"But they'll know," I began.

"They won't put it together, at least not right away, and that will give me time to go through the car before I turn it over to homicide."

"They won't like that," Simon cautioned. "They'll know you know better."

"Yeah, well, I'll play the distraught widow who can't think straight. And, hell, I'm old. That gives me a get-out-of-jail-free card most of the time."

"Wilma, let us take it from here," I pressed.

She smiled at me. "Not on your life, baby cakes. We're even partners in this one now. You find something, you let me know. If I find something, I'll return the favor. No charge either way. Deal?"

"Deal."

"Simon," she called out when we were at the door. "Watch her back. Sometimes she's got more guts than she's got smarts."

"I didn't know they made people like her any more," Simon stated as we slipped back into the traffic.

"I'm not sure they ever did."

I was somewhat irritated with Wilma and her

implication that Simon and I were a couple. I loved her but a little of her sometimes went a long way. She knew me just a bit too well. And what kind of men I liked. And she had no filter on that mouth of hers.

I glanced over at Simon. Those sparks Wilma was talking about with Al… I wondered if Simon felt any, because I certainly did every time he walked into a room and especially when he was no more than a foot away from me—like now. And when he touched me…

I needed a distraction. Now. Food was always good and we were way overdue for lunch.

"You hungry?" I asked. "How about some Kung Pao Chicken before you drop me off at my filming?"

I glanced over my shoulder at the traffic behind us. "There's a little restaurant up Rockville Pike. We could…"

My eyes settled on one car in particular.

"Do you see him?" Simon asked. "Beat-up black sedan two cars back." He stared hard at the rear view mirror. "I spotted it when we left the hospital parking lot. Then it disappeared, so I figured it was nothing, and now, hell if it hasn't shown back up."

I continued to look over the seat. It looked to be the same car that had caught my eye then, too. It was nondescript, easily missed, but I thought I recognized it as well.

"Don't stare. You're about as subtle as a brick, you know that?" Simon stated.

"*You're* the one driving a baby blue 1965 Mustang."

I turned back around and flopped back onto the seat. "If that's Isaacs, at least he doesn't know where you live, not if he had to stake out the hospital to find us."

"I suspect he doesn't know I exist. You didn't. But if that's him, he knows we're together now."

Suddenly Simon gunned the engine and swung a hard right through a yellow light, slinging me toward the gear shift.

"Power *out* of a curve, not into it," I instructed.

"I'm so glad I brought you along so you could tell me how to drive." He floored the pedal.

"This thing doesn't have air bags, does it?" I asked, bracing my feet.

"*You* drive a motorcycle."

"Right. The operative words are *I* drive."

At the next right, he squealed tires and swung right again, then sped up the next alley and bulldozed his way back onto the street we'd started on. The sedan was now up ahead of us, trapped in what was the beginning of rush hour traffic.

I flipped off my seatbelt and scooted out of the car, much to Simon's displeasure. The man actually yelled, "Hey!" at me as I took off running up the street. I dashed across the intersection, almost taking out a woman on five-inch stilettos, as the red hand flashed, daring me not to go. I made it just about to the next block before the sedan broke free and headed south toward the District. He knew we'd made him. We'd never find him, not with all the options he had.

I waited, leaning forward with my hands on my thighs, gasping for breath. It took Simon several more minutes before he pulled the Mustang up along side me.

"What was your plan? Were you going to splay yourself across his hood?" he asked, as I joined him.

"You would have loved that, wouldn't you?"

"It does have a certain appeal."

I swatted at him.

"Did you get anything?"

I held up a slip of paper. "Maryland tags. If it was Isaacs, the car is probably stolen. Still, I'd appreciate a little acknowledgment for my effort."

"Consider it acknowledged. Anything else?"

"It looked like a man driving."

"That rules out slightly more than half the population. Of course we already know Isaacs is male."

"I don't think it was Isaacs," I confessed.

"Why not?"

"The hair. It wasn't gray. Isaacs is what? Fifty something by now? Prison's hard on a person, even if he has good genes—which he doesn't. And Isaacs was pretty heavy into drug and alcohol abuse for years before he was sent up."

Simon looked over at me. "You think this guy was younger. There is a thing called hair dye, you know."

I knew. I also knew criminals frequently used disguises. Some even dressed as women to avoid detection. But something in my gut told me this guy drove like he was used to today's D.C. traffic—not what it'd been like fifteen years ago.

Simon pulled out his cell and hit speed dial.

"Manny, could you look up a tag for me?"

He read Manny the letters and numbers on the paper I'd handed him.

"Manny a friend of yours?" I asked. "From the Pittsburgh, P.D.?"

"Let's just say that wherever Manny may happen to be, he has access to a national data base of license plates. Also, in the weighing out of favors, he's got some catching up to do."

A minute later Manny came back on the line.

"Thanks," Simon said. "No, that doesn't even come close to evening the score. I'll be talking to you later."

Simon ended the call and tossed the phone between us.

We were out of the worst part of the traffic now and onto the I-270 spur towards Rockville and something to eat.

"So? Tell me." Patience was something I had little time for.

"Didn't Isaacs have a son?" Simon asked, watching me carefully.

"Yeah. Christopher. But why—"

"That sedan is registered to Christopher Isaacs."

My skin prickled, as I sank into the car seat under the weight of Simon's words. Christopher Isaacs, the little boy who was left to grow up without a father, had done just that.

And now he was tailing me.

"Hey, you all right over there?" Simon asked.

I didn't answer. The only sympathy I'd had for the Isaacs' family had been for Christopher. When I was contacting people about the documentary, I'd left him alone because I thought he deserved a life of his own. His father had already messed that life up sufficiently without my pounding home the fact.

But Christopher was grown now. He had to be somewhere in his mid-twenties. He was a man.

"Are psychopathic tendencies inherited?" I managed.

"Can be. I read that..."

I didn't hear the rest of what Simon was saying. My mind was racing. Christopher had to have major issues. But who did he blame for those issues? His father? Or people like me and Claire?

The game had just changed. I *knew* Luther Isaacs. But I didn't know Christopher. I had no idea what he was capable of. Or how deeply his hatred might run.

Or how badly he might want me dead.

Chapter 7

We ate but I had little appetite for anything after the Christopher Isaacs incident. Simon, on the other hand, was enjoying the hell out of some fiery concoction with red peppers that would have left welts on my lips for a week. Whatever served for his stomach had to be made out of something more akin to cast iron than living tissue.

"Someone will have to confront Christopher about why he was following us," I stated. I was past the main course, finishing an orange slice when the fortune cookies arrived with the bill. "I'm assuming you got an address with the name."

He nodded, savoring the last bit of fried rice on his plate. "I did, and by someone I take it you mean me."

"That would be helpful."

It was the last thing I personally wanted to do. If Christopher had somehow transferred the blame for how screwed up his life was to me—which certainly wouldn't be hard if he, too, was a psychopath—I had no desire to give him an opportunity to blow my head off.

"Okay, I agree a visit to Christopher might be productive," Simon said. "But what would I confront him with? He was driving on the public streets."

"He was *following* us."

"True, but we have no evidence he intended either of us harm. Frankly, I doubt he did."

Simon might be right, but my paranoia was in full bloom. Having my windows blown out and Claire shot at was enough to put almost anyone connected with Isaacs on the list of people who might want me dead. Christopher would have been worse than crazy to start anything on a crowded street. But at my home early this morning...

"Maybe confront is too strong a word," I said. "How about a simple conversation that includes a few questions."

"I'm open to suggestions."

"See if you can find out if he's had any contact with his father since Isaacs' release. And if he owns a shotgun. And how belligerent he is towards me and Claire. And what the hell he was doing following us."

"Okay. I'll see what I can do—if I can find him."

"Be careful," I said. "If Mary Ann was telling the truth and Isaacs isn't with her, he must be getting help from somebody. His son would be the obvious choice."

"I will be," he assured me.

I pulled out my phone and dialed Wes's number again. It rang until his voice mail picked up. "Call me, damn it" was all I said.

Disgusted, I shoved the phone back into my jeans pocket.

"Wes again?"

I nodded.

"I don't know how he can resist your charm."

"Trust me. Wes seems strangely immune to my charm when he's rattled."

"And you think that's why he's not responding to your calls? You think he's scared?"

"I hope that's it," I confessed.

"Know him well?"

"Sometimes I think I don't know him at all."

Simon nodded. He made no attempt to disguise his contempt for Wes, but there was still that hint of rivalry going on. Why? I had no idea. I shared Simon's contempt.

Still, I had to know where the hell Wes was. And why I had such bad feelings about what might have happened to him. I'd prefer to believe Wes was ignoring me rather than that he couldn't call me back.

"Aren't you going to call your producer?"

Darn it. I'd forgotten all about Conrad, not that he made it easy. He'd left me five or six messages on my cell phone.

I pulled up his number on my contact menu. He answered on the third ring.

"Conrad, I'm sorry I haven't gotten back to you about—"

"Hot damn, Eva. Have you seen the news? We can't buy publicity like this. Isaacs' photo is on every newscast on every channel. How soon can you get the film together?"

"I'm a little busy here, Conrad."

"Right. How are *you*?"

I could always trust Conrad to keep his priorities in order.

"At the moment, in one piece. So you don't need the raw footage?"

"No. Our backers released the money to me this morning. I've even had someone else call interested in buying in. Are you sure you can't speed up production?"

"Bye." I severed the connection.

"Something wrong?" Simon asked, reading the sour look that, I had no doubt, was all over my face.

"Nope. Everything's dandy. The only thing that might make the prospects for my documentary even better would be my death. Then Conrad would have a true runaway hit on his hands. Of course, that would present another minor problem for him. Who would make it?"

"You only need one person to see your finished product," he reminded me. "The district attorney."

I could feel my face soften. Simon knew exactly how I felt. I didn't care if the film didn't turn one dollar of profit. All I wanted was the reopening of the August Eight case.

"My cameraman's meeting me this afternoon at four at

the home of Edwina Jackson's granddaughter," I said. "I'd appreciate your dropping me off."

"Victim number six," Simon stated.

He knew them every bit as well as I did. I could still see the paragraph posted below her photo on the wall at his house. She was the grandmother who'd died while her grandchildren watched television inside her home.

"You think it's wise to continue with the interviews?" Simon asked.

"How would Isaacs or whoever's doing these shootings know the schedule for my interviews? Only my producer and my crew know that. Besides, we don't know that the attacks are in any way connected with the documentary."

Simon rolled his eyes.

"Okay, even if I give you that the documentary may be the focus, what could anybody—even Isaacs—have against Edwina's granddaughter?"

"What could anybody have against Claire?"

"She's a psychologist. She works with unstable people."

Simon didn't respond. He just looked at me. Who was I trying to kid? We both knew Claire was shot at because of this case. If she wasn't the direct target, my relationship with her made her one.

"Okay, point taken," I agreed. "But Debra was only nine years old when her grandmother died. It's not like she could testify against him."

"She heard the shots?"

"All three of the children did. They ran to the window but the car was gone. They all saw their grandmother lying dead on the sidewalk. Can you imagine? Debra was the oldest. She called 911."

"Rough for a little kid like that. And for a big kid like you."

He watched to see my reaction. But I refused to give

him one, swallowing to stop the tightening I felt in my throat. "*You* should know."

"I wasn't there. That makes it entirely different."

I studied him. The man exuded confidence. But his comment about Debra hinted at a softer side. I wondered if I could convince him to let me interview him on camera. He would certainly make the female part of my audience take notice, and I would love to get some answers he might not otherwise give me.

"Tell me about your brother," I said softly, avoiding eye contact as I ate the last orange slice and then wiped the juice from my fingers with the hot washcloth our waiter had brought.

He stiffened as his walls immediately went up, the warmth disappearing from his demeanor. "Here's the deal: You don't ask me about Michael, and I won't ask you about David." His eyes held mine, challenging my response.

"All right," I agreed. It wasn't as though the subject was up for discussion.

It'd been fifteen years. I could talk about David if he wanted, despite the guilt and the hurt. I was good with the talk, not so good with dealing with the residuals. Claire's group had given me the openness, but I think time would have given me that, too. Why this reaction?

I cracked open my fortune cookie. *A wise man never puts all his cards on the table.* Maybe I'd just gotten my answer.

Ben, my cameraman, was in the van sorting through his equipment when Simon dropped me off at Debra's. Ben's relief was obvious in his grin.

"Damn. I wasn't sure you were going to show after what I heard on the news," he offered. He would have hugged me if he'd dared.

Ben was cheeriness bottled. He even had the round cheeks of a chipmunk to go with it. A year or two younger than me, he looked a good five older. He had a beer gut that had less to do with beer and more to do with potato chips, and favored plaid shirts worn unbuttoned over rock band T-shirts.

He was also incredibly talented and had an uncanny ability to read my facial cues during an interview and know exactly what I wanted at any given moment—a closeup, me and the interviewee together, or a larger shot of the room. I'd known him four years. He was expensive and worth every penny. I'd missed him last week when he was sick and Wes was filling in. Wes's work was a mere shadow of Ben's.

"Are you feeling okay?" I asked.

"Yeah. It must have been some kind of intestinal flu or maybe it was something I ate. Wes and I went bar hopping. I had a whole lot of Buffalo wings and those nuts and pretzels they put out in those little bowls. Who knows what I picked up."

Ben's friendship with Wes had always been a mystery to me. They were about as different as two people could be. But Wes did attract women, and maybe that was what Ben liked about going out with him.

"You're sure you're all right now," I asked.

"Count on it."

"I've also got the interview you did with Jesse Sedwick week before last transferred to a DVD," Ben added. "And the one with Dennis Toro's son. Remember to take them with you when we finish."

Dennis Toro, an immigrant from the Philippines, had been in this country for little more than a decade when he was gunned down. He never got to see his six children grow up. His oldest son had expanded the little magazine kiosk Dennis had run at the mall into an independent bookstore in Rockville. I'd conducted my interview with him there, in front of a display he was preparing for Veterans' Day.

"Are we about ready?" I asked Ben.

"Oh, yeah, just waiting for your approval."

He'd already been inside, scoping out the best place to film with Debra who had just come off her nursing shift at the hospital. He knew what I wanted: the spot where my subject was most comfortable. The room, the corner, the couch—whatever evoked the personality I'd be working with. For Debra Jackson Roddy, that meant her kitchen table.

Ben had the lights set up and the sound equipment in place. He brought in the camera and the tripod after I gave him the okay.

Debra sliced me a piece of apple pie, even warmed it for me in the microwave, poured me a glass of milk, and served it to me there at the table. It smelled absolutely incredible.

"I shouldn't be eating this," I confessed, as I took a bite. It was just about the most delicious thing I had ever put in my mouth.

"Grandma used to say anything made with love can't do a person any harm. That's her recipe. It's my way of acknowledging that she's here with us, helping us along, making us strong. I wanted you to feel her presence, too."

I did but it was through this extraordinarily strong woman that Edwina had left as her legacy.

Debra played with the fringe on her place mat as she watched me eat, obviously nervous.

"Do you remember that evening?" I asked.

"Do I remember? For years it was all I remembered, all I thought about, all I dreamed about. You know what I mean. You dreamed, too, didn't you?"

I nodded. For me, the dreams had never completely stopped. Just when I thought they had, I'd have another one. And since I'd started work on the documentary, they'd come more often, almost every day.

"The day after it happened," Debra said, "I woke up convinced my grandmother's death was all a dream, that she was still alive. I ran down the stairs to tell my mother and stopped at the bottom step. Grandma's portrait was on a table in front of the window, draped in black. It was real." Her eyes shone with tears. "That was really, really hard."

My throat constricted. I wanted to touch her hand, but I didn't want my emotions on film, and I wanted desperately to get Debra's honesty recorded.

"Can you tell us about the day your grandmother died?" I asked.

"Let me first share with you how she lived." Debra's eyes grew large as a sweet, sad smile lifted her mouth.

This was exactly what I'd hoped for. I needed it all. Edwina's life, her death, her children and grandchildren's loss. I needed the impact of that bullet that took her life brought onto film. If there was any chance we could arouse enough public interest to put pressure on the district attorney to reopen the case, this would be how we'd do it. Present the victims in the fullness of their lives, then show what death did to those left behind. I intended for it to be like the before and after pictures from a tornado or a hurricane. The devastation was every bit as real, but so much harder to assess. And so very impossible to repair.

"Tell us," I said.

"She worked at the florist every morning, but she watched us kids every day after school until our mother got home from work. She always had cake or cookies and milk waiting for us at the table as soon as we hopped off the bus. Then it was homework time. And after that we could play games or watch a little TV while she prepared supper. We minded her—all of us. We knew just what she expected from us and we didn't give her any sass. If we did, she'd sit us down and put the fear of the Lord in us." She shook her head. "It wasn't the Lord we feared, it was disappointing her."

"And the day she died..."

"Mom had something special she had to do at church, so she'd dropped us kids off for a couple of hours at

Grandma's. We were in the back room watching a video. Grandma had left us for just a minute. I didn't even know she'd stepped out to sweep the sidewalk, but it was such a beautiful evening and I suspect she just wanted a breath of fresh air. We were never allowed to play in the front yard. She said there was too much traffic.

"I heard the shot, but I wasn't sure what it was. All the kids jumped up to see. The front door was open. I looked through the screen and I saw her lying there on the concrete, the broom on the ground next to her. I knew it was bad, even though I couldn't see any blood. I told my sister to take the younger kids to the back room. Then I went outside but I...I couldn't go near her. I knew she was dead. I ran back inside, slammed the door and locked it to make sure none of the other kids went out there. Then I called 911.

"I tried to keep the kids away from the picture window while we waited for the police to arrive, but I couldn't. They wanted to help her."

I placed my hand over Debra's as she continued to talk, Ben filmed, and all three of us cried.

When Simon picked me up from Debra's house, I was still shaken, but he didn't seem to notice. He was not a happy man.

"That woman is certifiably nuts," Simon insisted, even before I could get the door open to get into the car.

"What woman?" I asked, climbing in next to him and glad for a distraction. "I thought you were going to check out Christopher's address."

"Seems Christopher lives with his mother. Or did. That's her address on the car's registration."

Ah, yes, Angela. I'd never met the woman, but I'd take Simon's word for it. She had to have been a little strange to ever take up with the likes of Isaacs.

"I take it you didn't find Christopher."

"She said she hasn't seen him in over a week."

My heart quickened. So Isaacs and Christopher probably were working together. "Not since Isaacs got out of prison?"

"Precisely," Simon agreed. "She told him that if he saw his father, he didn't need to bother coming back home."

"And Christopher took her at her word."

"Apparently."

"At least she talked to you."

"Not really. I got all of that from her rant when I asked to see her son. Then she told me to get the hell off her property and threatened to call the police."

"Did you tell her you *are* the police?"

He nodded, keeping his eyes on the traffic. "When I showed her my badge, she offered to shoot me and anybody else who came around uninvited. If I'd wait just a moment, she'd go and get her gun and prove it to me."

I suppressed the smile I felt forming on my lips. It wasn't as if Angela had been any real threat to Simon, but she certainly had rattled him. He hadn't planned to upset her. And I doubt that he had. He'd simply caught the brunt of her distress. And that was sad, too. He felt sorry for her. Still, the thoughts of her threatening this tall, powerful man was something else.

"I take it you didn't wait for her to get her gun."

He didn't bother answering.

"Think I'd have any better luck talking to her?" I asked.

"You might, but I don't want you anywhere near her. The woman's dangerous."

And maybe she was. Or maybe she was just hurting. I wasn't sure how to feel about Angela Isaacs. She'd picked Luther to father her son, a decision that would forever influence her life. She should have taken time to find out what Isaacs was like before she'd slept with him.

The thought brought me up short. Maybe Angela and I

weren't as different as I'd like to believe, not if I'd slept with Simon the first day I'd met him. Something had happened between us the first time I'd been at his house. I'd told him about Claire, probably about Jackie, maybe even about Wes. He may have told me about Michael as well. Sharing that kind of tragedy created a sense of trust, vulnerability, and intimacy. Sometimes it was warranted. Sometimes not.

But if I *had* slept with Simon, he was no Isaacs. Still, I couldn't help but wonder if my actions would have consequences as well. Was I letting my attraction to Simon skew my objectivity?

I shook my thoughts from my mind and tried to stay focused on Christopher.

"I'll ask Wilma if she knows somebody we can get to watch Angela's house. That way, if Christopher turns up, we can get a tail on him."

"You really think he'll go back there?"

"She's his mother. He'll show up eventually. He must still have belongings there."

But even as I said those words, I felt certain that if Christopher had been in the car that had followed us, we would probably see him before Angela would. I wondered where he was staying.

"I need my Jeep," I said. "Think you can drop me by my house?"

My motorcycle was my preferred mode of transportation, but not when it was cold, and we'd been close to frost last night.

"You sure?" Simon asked. I could see the concern in his face.

"You can't keep playing chauffeur for me. You must have had a life before you met me."

He continued to stare at me, not answering.

"What's the matter? You think Isaacs is going to have staked out the crime scene that is my house? He's bold, but come on."

"I just don't want you lulled into thinking it might be all right to stay there tonight. Your security system isn't working and won't be until a couple of days after your door and windows are replaced."

I considered that for a moment. I hadn't given much thought as to where I'd sleep. Jackie's husband really wouldn't appreciate my staying with her. And Claire was at the hospital. I wasn't about to go to Jesse and Nina's. There really wasn't anywhere else short of a hotel and that had its own problems.

"Are you making me an offer?" I asked.

"You might call it a proposition."

He openly enjoyed the look of embarrassment on my face.

"I propose that you feel free to make my home yours for as long as you need to."

He suddenly became very serious. "This isn't over. You know that, Eva. I'd just feel better if you were with me."

My smart remark about Chateau Talbot died on my lips. I knew he was right. I could take care of myself, or so I'd tried to convince myself for fifteen years. But four hands were certainly better than two. I'd feel safer with him.

"All right. I'll spend tonight at your house. But this doesn't mean I'm going to impose upon you for long."

"Fine. Just as long as I know you're all right. We can take this one day at a time. Trust me, Eva."

Trust was not my issue. It never had been. It was one of my flaws, as both Jackie and Jesse frequently pointed out. I trusted people a little too quickly, which was one of the reasons I'd married two too many men. But I refused to let my critics change me. My world was dark enough without taking away what little faith I had left in humanity.

I'd also learned to trust people to act in character, which meant I was good at anticipating how personalities would interact. After we finished at my house, I had one more stop to make: Wes's apartment. And I needed to go alone. I doubted I would find him at home, but putting Wes and Simon together would be an invitation to a testosterone standoff. And I certainly didn't need Wes questioning my relationship with Simon once I did find him. Wes had a possessive streak where I was concerned, and I knew which one I'd rather have watching my back. Whatever had happened Sunday night, Wes had left me. And I had to know why.

Chapter 8

"Geez, what a mess," I muttered to Simon, kicking a stray shard of glass across my kitchen floor. My contractor had had his men sweep up, but they hadn't gotten it all. "I'll be picking slivers of glass out of my bare feet for the next six months."

"If that's your only problem..." Simon began.

Indeed, glass on the floor was the smallest part of the damage. Splinters had been torn from my beautiful rattan furniture, and the cotton fabric of the cushions had been pitted.

I turned and took a good look at the half wall below my kitchen counter. There were pellet-sized holes torn in the sheet rock. "Did you see this?" I asked.

"Better the wall than our skin."

"Better nothing at all."

I could simply replace the furniture, but the thought of all the repairs that had to be done made my head hurt. I spied a place where a chunk of granite had been taken out of the counter. "This place looks like a bomb went off in here."

A big thump on the deck caught my attention, and I turned to see the repairmen lift the last piece of plywood into place. It blocked out the setting sun and left only the kitchen light to illuminate the sitting area.

"See? It's looking better already," Simon ribbed.

"Right. Once the kitchen light goes out, we can pretend everything's normal."

There was a knock at the front door and I opened it. Thomas Jennings, the T J in T J Contracting, was standing on my front stoop. "We'll be out of here in about ten minutes," he said. "What we've put up should be secure for now. I've already ordered the new windows and door."

"When will you have them?"

"I put a rush on it. Maybe tomorrow, but most likely the day after that. Once I've got them, I'll schedule their installation."

"Okay. And when you get them up—"

"I'll see to it that the security system is repaired as well."

"And the inside work?"

"Next week at the earliest. I'm booked solid. I had to blow off a job to get people over here for you today."

"Thanks, Tom."

"Sure. You be careful now." He tipped his baseball cap at me and left.

I shut the door after him, wondering if Tom thought my not being "careful" was the reason someone had shot up my kitchen.

Simon came up behind me. "So, are you going to follow me home in your Jeep?"

"No. I've got a few things I have to do. My first stop is my bedroom closet."

"Good idea. You'll need a few clean clothes."

"That, too. Thanks for reminding me."

He followed me to the bedroom and watched as I opened a tall cabinet inside my walk-in closet. I pulled out a large satchel and loaded it with ammunition, an automatic, a sawed off shotgun, a couple of canisters of pepper spray, and a stun gun.

"If you put stakes and holy water in there, I'm out of here," Simon said over my shoulder.

"I would if I thought they would help, but our foe is all too human."

"Do you have permits for any of that?"

"Don't ask questions you don't want to know the

answers to."

"You do know sawed off shotguns are illegal throughout the United States."

"Don't you have something else you could do right now?" I asked, adding more ammunition to my bag.

"You're out of my jurisdiction so your misdemeanors are safe with me, but federal offenses… Surely you don't think you're going to need all of that."

I shook my head. "Most of it's for show. I'd rather scare the hell out of Isaacs or whoever shot at us than actually take him down. I have no problem with him spending the rest of his natural life in jail. But in the event that's not an option…"

"Point taken."

I grabbed a few clothes, stuffed them on top of my supplies, and zipped the satchel shut. When I turned, Simon was studying the photos over the mantel of the small gas fireplace to the left of my bed.

"Who's the guy in the camouflage?"

"That would be mistake number one."

"Ah. The ex-husband."

"There were two actually."

"This one was military?"

"Not exactly. I met Barry when I took a course in evasive driving. He was the instructor. He's a man of many talents, most of which, I realized after we were married, are up for sale."

"Mercenary?"

The look on his face was priceless. It'd been the same expression I'd seen on my dad's face when I told him I was marrying Barry. If my mother had still been alive, I never would have done it, even though I'd been twenty-four. That was the only good thing to come out of the loss of my parents: the freedom not to care what anybody thought of me.

"Mercenary has such a negative connotation," I said. "Barry preferred soldier of fortune."

"You actually *married* a *soldier of fortune?*"

"Not the kind that advertises in the back of gun magazines. He doesn't do anything he's morally opposed to, and, believe it or not, he was a nice guy. Still is. I learned a lot from him."

He shook his head. I knew exactly how odd that sounded, but emotions are complex and how we play them out can sometimes be a bit bizarre. I was sure I didn't have to explain that to him.

"Your Barry sounds more like someone who should be given a wide berth."

"Only if you're on his bad side."

"Then why aren't the two of you still married?"

I paused. "This is *so* none of your business."

"You're right, it's not. But let me guess. You married him because he had an air of danger about him and you were tired of feeling numb. And he made you feel safe."

I was not playing this game, especially when Simon was so good at it.

"And you divorced him because... What? You didn't feel scared anymore?"

His words brought me up short. The world continued to be an unpredictable and dangerous place for me. But maybe Simon was right. I wasn't scared anymore. I'd done everything I could think of to gain some control over my existence. Isn't that what fear was all about, a lack of control?

"I divorced Barry because my fears were no foundation for a marriage. Life comes at us. You can either get in the game or not. One thing you can't do is send in a surrogate for you."

"How long did it last?"

"Less than a year."

"And ex number two?"

"Haven't I shaken your faith in my judgment sufficiently?"

"You're an interesting woman, Eva. You're not afraid of life."

I considered that a moment. I don't suppose I was. What I feared was having that life snatched from me by some maniac before I was finished with it.

"My second marriage lasted almost two years, probably because he was away most of the time. He was with the CIA."

"Another risk taker."

"Only this one had questionable ethics. Very effective, but a little too hot on the ends justifying the means.

"So how about you?" I asked. "You ever been married?"

He shook his head. "I can barely take care of myself."

I laughed out loud.

"Seriously. I can't cook anything except chili and hot dogs, but I do warm up a mean leftover pizza. When I do laundry, everything comes out the same color, and if a woman awakens me out of a dead sleep, I'm likely to put a gun to her head."

"Ever the charmer, aren't you? Tell me, have there been lots of hers?"

"Enough."

Simon's gaze shifted to a smaller silver frame.

"You still keep his photo up."

He was referring to David. I knew he would see it, but I'd hoped he wouldn't say anything. It was a picture of the two of us at Hershey Park in front of a giant chocolate kiss. We'd asked a passerby to take it. David had his arms around me. Both of us were laughing, reveling in the bliss of young love. He'd been good to me. Loving, kind, thoughtful, almost too perfect. And at the moment the shutter had snapped, we'd thought we had years ahead of us to learn about life, to explore what love was all about. The photo had been taken three weeks before David had been killed. Sometimes I felt as though it'd been taken in an alternate universe.

"The love of your life," Simon stated. He'd taken it off the mantel and was holding the frame in his hand.

"No. That's the problem."

Simon turned and I met his gaze head on. "I had just told David I was breaking up with him minutes before he was killed."

I had never told anyone that before, not my parents, not my friends, not even the members of Claire's support group. I wondered why I felt it necessary to tell Simon now. Maybe it was simply time.

"That's why it's so hard," he said.

"Yes."

I grabbed the heavy satchel and turned away, blinking back tears as I headed out of the room before he could say, 'You were only seventeen,' or 'You couldn't have known,' or whatever other platitude that might have come out of his mouth.

A boy I would have forgotten in a couple of months had given his life for mine. Now I could never forget him. And I could never love him. What kind of twisted irony was that? David deserved better. And so did I.

Simon followed me back into the hallway to the front door.

"I'll see you at your house later," I assured him, as I knelt at the coat closet and gathered up all the footage we'd shot so far, deliberately keeping my face turned away from his. I might find time to go over some of it at Simon's.

I went farther down the hallway, and, with my hand on the door to the garage, called back over my shoulder. "I don't know what time I'll get to your house, so don't bother cooking."

I heard Simon mutter, "And I was planning a nice Beef Wellington."

I lucked into a guest parking spot in the lot in front of Wes's complex. The six apartments in his building shared a hallway and were stacked in threes, each upon the other. Wes's was in the middle, with a basement apartment below. I took a thorough survey of the lot as I got out of my Jeep. Wes's car was nowhere to be seen.

His blinds were closed and I saw no light coming from any of the windows as I climbed the stairs and let myself into the hallway. His door was just inside to my right. There was no newspaper waiting to be picked up, not that I really thought Wes would take the *Post* or the *Times*. And whatever mail he might have was neatly concealed within the metal box with his name on it to the left of his door, so I couldn't tell if he'd been by to pick it up. In other words, there was nothing whatsoever to indicate when Wes might last have been here.

"Wes, open the door," I demanded, pounding on his door. I waited a couple of minutes and then tried again. "We need to talk, Wes. Let me in." Still nothing.

I rang the bell on his neighbor's door which stood just across the narrow hall and got no response. I knew someone was inside because I'd seen the lights on when I walked up the steps. So I called through the door.

"I'm Eva Keller, a friend of Wes Gallagher. Maybe you've seen me before when I came by to visit."

Not likely. I'd never visited Wes, but I had picked him up for one of the shoots last week.

"I'm trying to locate him," I called through the door.

My guess was whoever was inside was looking through the peephole. Except for my biker jacket, I looked about as innocuous as anybody could.

A young African-American woman opened the door, a shy toddler with big brown eyes wrapped around her leg.

"Is something wrong?" she asked.

"I don't think so. I'm just looking for Wes. Have you seen him since yesterday afternoon?"

She shook her head. "You his girlfriend or something?"

"Or something. You haven't heard him come or go? His door open or shut?"

Again, she shook her head and then looked me up and down. "If you're lookin' to be more than 'or something', you should probably know that Wes is a player. He has women in and out of his place all the time."

The little girl wrapped around her leg asked for a cracker.

"I gotta go."

"Thanks."

The door shut in my face.

So Wes wasn't just ducking my calls, at least not the ones to his land line. He hadn't come home last night. I had to know what happened Sunday night. I *had* to find him. But how?

I hopped back into my Jeep and made a quick call to a nearby restaurant to order takeout. It was the least I could do for my host. After I picked it up, I took off again toward Simon's with the aroma of North Carolina barbecue filling the air and teasing my appetite.

By now the rush hour had passed, leaving the narrow lanes of the tree-lined George Washington Parkway a peaceful drive as it curved along the Potomac in the dark until bright lights shone in my rear view mirror.

It was something large, maybe a Hummer, maybe a Suburban, built high enough to blind me with the headlights, especially with high beams. Whatever it was, it didn't like the fact that I was in front of it. I was already pushing the speed limit past what I should, especially on that curvy road. I sped up anyway, but the monster on my tail sped up, too, so close I would have sworn I had him in tow.

I swerved into the right lane so he could pass, but the monster followed me. He needed to go on around because we'd be narrowing to one lane soon as an entrance lane came onto the highway.

Metal screeched against metal as the impact from behind thrust me and my Jeep forward in a surge of speed. I grabbed hard onto the wheel, fighting to keep the machine on the pavement. I pulled hard to the left, bouncing into the next lane and speeding up again to put distance between us, hoping he'd either go on around me or get the hell off the highway.

Again the bumper behind plowed into my Jeep like a bulldozer, flinging me forward toward the steering wheel, my seatbelt strap burrowing into my chest.

I floored the pedal. The needle on the speedometer surged past ninety.

But the monster was even faster. He pulled up beside me and steered into me, ramming the right side of my car hard. The metal of the passenger door crumpled in a screech of protest as the window frosted over into a thousand pieces of glass. Thank goodness it held together, but my visibility was seriously impaired. I slammed on my brakes and pulled back into the lane behind the machine. The license plate had been removed, but I could see the make. It was, indeed, a hummer, a dark one.

The brake lights suddenly shone bright. I braked hard as well, ducking into the left lane. I was not about to be suckered into a head on collision. Barry had taught me better than that. I nicked the left corner of the bumper ahead with my own and skidded, almost losing control, but I pulled out of it, finding myself again to the right.

And then he was behind me again. The lane I was in turned abruptly into an exit lane. I'd never make the curve at that speed if I tried to escape off the road. And if I stayed where I was, I would plow headfirst into the bridge support.

I floored the pedal and swung the Jeep back into the left lane and ahead of the Hummer. Somehow I managed to keep the Jeep on the road as I passed under the bridge. Headlights flashed from the right. A car was entering the highway from the merge lane. There was nowhere for him to go.

One final surge from behind caught my bumper on its right corner. I couldn't turn right. I had no time to look left. I simply pulled the wheel hard. The Jeep plunged into the guard rail. It went into a spin, slinging me and it, airborne, into the median. I don't know why it didn't flip. Or how I managed to keep from plowing into the opposing lanes. All I know is that when the Jeep came down on the grass, all the airbags exploded around me and the engine suddenly died. I was trapped in a billow of white, wondering how I could possibly still be alive. My whole body shook. But I couldn't let my guard down.

As the airbags deflated, I forced my head up and looked out. In the dark I could make out a car stopped on the side of the road. I broke free from my seatbelt and fumbled frantically for the gun in my jacket pocket. I managed to pull it out, but my hands seemed detached from my body. My heart in my throat, I turned again toward the car behind me. I squinted at it and felt the tightness in my chest ease slightly. Whatever make the car was, it was a heck of a lot smaller than what had pushed me off the road.

A man shone a flashlight, startling me, as he tapped against my window.

"You all right in there?"

"I'm fine," I managed to call back.

The light darted around the interior of my Jeep and then flicked over me.

"Good God, lady. There's blood everywhere."

What was he talking about? Then I saw it, too, in the beam of his light. Red. Everywhere. On my arms, across the seat, on the roof, smearing the dashboard. If I'd lost that much blood, shouldn't I be in more pain?

I wiped at a spot on my arm, looking desperately for the source of the bleeding. But the blood had a strange texture. It was thicker than it should be. I touched a drop to my lips. Spicy. I shook my head with relief. Simon wouldn't be getting North Carolina barbeque for dinner tonight.

Chapter 9

"You look like hell," Simon said as he came down the back steps of his house.

"Just give me the twenty."

He handed me the bill, and I shoved it through the window of the cab at the driver as Simon unloaded both my duffle bag and my film bag from the trunk of the cab.

"Keep the change."

"You need a keeper, you know that?" Simon said, shouldering both bags as the cab executed a three-point turn and drove away. He'd said exactly the same thing when I'd called him twenty minutes ago from the body shop where I'd had my Jeep towed.

"Yeah, well if you're not applying for the job, keep your comments to yourself."

Avoiding eye contact, I pushed past him and headed up the steps. I didn't need a lecture.

"I would have come to get you," he said, following after me.

"A cab was faster."

He dumped the bags on the porch, grabbed my arm and spun me around, forcing me to look into his eyes. "Stop it. Eva, someone just tried to kill you."

I tried to choke back the tears but they had already started, and I was almost too weak to stand. I collapsed into his arms, everything within me pouring out through my sobs. Years of grief and fear exploded from somewhere deep inside me. But mostly it was the terror, not of dying but of being a victim, of becoming one more number in a long list, and the horror that the murderer would win, that he would kill again.

I would not let him win. I would not. I found myself pounding on Simon's chest.

I tried to pull back, swiping at my tears, but Simon held me fast, crushing me against him, protecting me within his embrace. I struggled and then gave into it, letting him, at least for a few moments, take on the task.

He kissed my hair as he uttered soft, soothing sounds so low that I couldn't make out the words. Simon scooped me up and carried me inside, up the stairs, and into the bedroom. He lay me gently on the bed and pulled off my jacket. He disappeared for several moments and then returned with a warm, wet washcloth that he drew across my cheeks, dabbing at my eyes, washing away the traces of my tears.

He leaned down and gently kissed my lips. Then my cheeks, my eyes, and my neck.

I drew him hungrily to me, kissing him hard on the mouth, his lips parting, his passion as greedy as my own. We couldn't get close enough to each other. His scent, the feel of his skin—I wanted to feel alive.

He pulled back. "I don't want to hurt you."

"I'm fine," I assured him, pulling him closer again.

He nuzzled my neck, gently dropping kisses as he outlined my collar bone. He pulled up my T-shirt, kissing each portion of skin as it was exposed and then drew it over my head. He was back at my neck, nibbling my ears and again finding my mouth.

I broke loose and tugged at his T-shirt. Quickly it was gone, exposing the muscles that had been hidden beneath it. I pulled him to me, wanting to feel every inch of his skin against my own.

"What happened Saturday night? After we came back here." I whispered in his ear.

He drew back just enough so I could see his smile as he looked into my eyes.

"I'll show you," he promised.

I slept for almost two hours, relaxed, my mind free for the first time since I could remember. Then I found myself abruptly awake, lying on my side on the queen-size bed. I reached out and felt strangely relieved. Simon was resting on the other side.

I pushed myself up on my elbow, supporting my head with my hand. I smiled as I watched him sleep, tempted to wake him for another round of lovemaking, but that wouldn't be fair. He needed his rest.

He looked younger asleep, his features reflecting the glow from the streetlight outside the window. The lines had softened across his forehead and around his eyes. He seemed relaxed for the first time since I'd been with him.

I wondered what he was dreaming. A frown suddenly contorted his face, and I didn't want to know. He shifted but didn't wake. I had my demons and Simon had his. To pretend otherwise was dangerous. So was deluding myself that the monsters we battled within were no barrier to a relationship.

I rolled over and faced the window. I needed to sleep, too, if I could. I closed my eyes.

Blood spews from David's chest, as I cradle his head in my lap. I can feel it soaking through the cotton of my skirt. I press my hands into the wound and try desperately to stop the flow, but my hands turn red, and I can no longer tell where the wound is.

"Don't die, don't die, don't die," I beg. But David doesn't answer. His eyes are closed.

I pull his head against my chest and rock him in my arms. I can feel the life seeping from him, as my tears wash over both of our cheeks.

"Don't leave me," I plead.

Men in white shirts and blue pants are standing over us. "Please, miss, let us help him."

> But I don't let go. If I do, David will die. Why don't they understand?
>
> They pull him out of my arms. "You've killed him," I gasp. I look down where David's body had lain and see nothing but blood. My hands, my arms, my dress—all covered in David's blood.

I sat straight up in bed, my heart pounding and my chest heaving. I was wide awake and drenched in sweat. I threw back the covers and swung my bare legs out over the side of the bed, as I forced myself to calm.

I looked back at Simon. He was still asleep, and I didn't want to wake him. I pulled on my clothes and went downstairs. I wouldn't be sleeping anymore tonight, not if there was any chance I'd dream about David.

I would have liked to leave the house, but I no longer had wheels. I couldn't scour the area for the Hummer with the red paint of my Jeep embedded in its bumper unless I did it on my none-too-subtle motorcycle. I'd have to leave that to the police. There'd been no license plate, and I couldn't even swear the Hummer was black. Besides, I was sure it would have been abandoned, not a hair, a fiber, or a fingerprint left anywhere.

I did, however, have other things to occupy my mind—mainly Al's notes. Al was meticulous. That was one of the reasons I'd hired him. Not only was he good at deduction, he had an eye for detail, and he recorded everything, including things he and most everyone else would dismiss as irrelevant. He always said, "You just never know."

I took over Simon's tiny kitchen table and the single chair I suspected he never used. Working helped to distract me from the thoughts that had drifted through my mind in the night. That's where worry lay. Action needed light, and action was my only solution to the problem of whoever it was that wanted me dead.

Several hours later I heard the water running in the upstairs bathroom. Simon was up. By the time his step creaked on the stairs, I'd already gone through Al's notes and photos several times, hoping to find something I might have missed.

"There's coffee in the pot," I called out.

My coffee making skills might not be the best, but I was getting a good surge of caffeine from my mug, and, as far as I was concerned, that was pretty much all that coffee was good for.

"Hell, woman, did you get *any* sleep?"

The almost empty coffee carafe, juice bottles, and milk carton were a dead giveaway as to how long I'd been up. So, I suspected, were the bags under my eyes and the condition of the tank top and sweat pants that I was wearing.

I looked up and he bent to give me a quick kiss on the lips.

"You're getting water on me," I protested.

"Sorry about that."

I watched as he rubbed a towel over his face, droplets glistening in his hair and on his broad shoulders from his shower.

I took in the view with an appreciative sweep. No shirt, just jeans. Really nice pecs and abs, and, of course, there were those biceps. Was he trying to distract me? Well, it wouldn't work, at least not right now.

I dropped my gaze back to the papers in front of me, allowing myself only an occasional, surreptitious glance.

"Oh, and there's a box of doughnuts on the counter next to the fridge." It was the least I could do for a man who had washed away my tears last night.

And one who seemed intent on keeping me alive. Besides, neither one of us had gotten any of that North Carolina barbecue that had most likely permanently adhered itself to the interior of what was left of my Jeep.

"I didn't take you for the doughnut type," he said with an appreciative glance of his own. He already had one of the blueberry cake in his hand.

"I'm not usually, but I figured you were," I bluffed.

"Right. That's why three are already missing."

A lot of hours had passed during the night, and the only place open at four in the morning had been the doughnut shop on the corner. I'd needed a break and some fresh air. And I deserved at least three doughnuts, maybe four, after what I'd been through.

"Al documented Mary Ann picking up Isaacs at the prison, sans her children whom she apparently left at her ex's. She took him out to eat at a steak house buffet, where they spent close to three hours, and then home with her. Al stayed until the lights went out about midnight. Isaacs was still at the house when Al got back there the next morning by seven o'clock. He'd pulled in a second agent for the night shift. I've got his notes, too, but he saw no activity whatsoever."

"Or he slept through it."

That was always a possibility with a stake-out, especially when only one agent was involved, frequently a cop who had just come off a twelve-hour shift. But I was banking on Al's having employed only the best for me. He knew how I felt about Isaacs.

What I had weren't Al's final reports, simply his notes. Scribbled in with everything else was a list of what he ate: a number 4 combo from McDonald's for lunch that Wilma had brought him with a note not to repeat McDonald's for supper. God love him, Al must have been worried about his arteries. Had he known what the weekend would bring, he wouldn't have cared.

Thinking about Al made me want another doughnut. One never knew. And somehow I thought Al would appreciate the thought.

I flipped through the pages. "That week Isaacs went

pretty much nowhere other than to an appointment with a dentist in the company of his sister." I sat up straighter. "But he did have a visitor."

"Let me guess. Christopher."

"Right on the first try. Christopher's sedan, with the matching plates we recorded, appeared at Mary Ann's home four times that week: the day of Isaacs' release, twice on the following Wednesday, and again on Friday."

I passed over a photo of Christopher and another of his sedan. He was a nice looking kid. Thin, dark-haired. I wondered if he resembled his mother. He looked very little like his dad.

"Did Isaacs ever leave with him?"

"No. Then Saturday evening Isaacs left—alone—in his sister's car a little after seven o'clock."

"About the time you went to meet Wes in Dupont."

"Right. Al followed him to the same bar where I met with Wes and where you were. He had trouble parking. He finally got a space a couple of streets over. Al watched him enter the bar a little after eight fifteen, but he was only inside a minute or two. He came back out, got back into the car, and drove to his sister's where he remained the rest of the night."

"Anything else in his notes about Sunday?"

I shook my head. "If there was anything on Sunday, the notes would have been in Al's car or on his person. We already know nothing was found on his body. I'll call Wilma later and ask if anything might have turned up anywhere else."

"Isaacs must have seen me with you and Wes." Simon leaned back against the counter. The way he was eating those doughnuts, I should have bought a second dozen.

"Likely," I agreed. "Of course, we're assuming, without any real proof, that Wes had somehow been in contact with him, and he had come there to meet with me. Tell me again what happened at the bar, and this time I want all the details."

"I saw you join Wes at a table."

"Where were you?"

"At the bar."

"Alone?"

"Yes. The two of you talked, and you didn't seem at all pleased with him."

Wes must have been stalling about telling me why he'd asked me to come.

"He gave you something," Simon added, "and you seemed a little less unhappy with him."

My dad's medal.

"I recognized you from your photos," Simon explained, "and decided to come over and introduce myself."

"In the middle of an argument?"

"I didn't want to have to arrest you for disturbing the peace."

"So your badge works in D.C. now? How did you know who I was?"

"I read an article in the *Post* about your documentaries and your newest project, which I obviously have a personal stake in. Your photo was with it."

The interview had come out last week, one of my producer's coups designed to impress our backers.

"So you just happened to be in that bar when I was with Wes."

"Serendipity."

I wasn't buying it. "Why were you there?"

"They have the best selection of on-tap beer in the D.C. area."

He could have been telling the truth. Or not. There was nothing in his demeanor for me to read. I'd asked twice and he'd answered. I wouldn't get more right now, which reinforced my determination to go by the bar. The thought crossed my mind that Simon might somehow have known Isaacs would be there. But that seemed unlikely.

Or that he might have followed Wes.

Or me.

But why would he?

"You must have scared off Isaacs."

"Maybe. I can tell you that Wes wanted me gone."

Wes would have wanted Simon gone even if he hadn't arranged a meeting with Isaacs. He would have sensed the attraction between us, and he would have been jealous. Wes was like that, even though there'd been nothing physical between us for many years. Had it distracted him from what we were there for? Wes was easily distracted.

But I wasn't. If Wes had arranged a meeting with Isaacs, why hadn't he told me when he called me? Was he afraid I'd refuse to meet with him? I'm not sure, even now, what I would have done if Isaacs had showed up unannounced. I might have tried to deck him.

My best guess was that Wes wanted to feel valuable to me. I'm pretty sure he must have told me we were waiting for Isaacs. If he hadn't, I would have left as soon as I'd gotten Dad's medal.

"But you didn't leave the bar," I said.

"Are you kidding me? Walk away from the love of my life?"

"What?" The word slipped out of my mouth before I saw the playful grin on his handsome face.

"It was like a meteor shower, the fourth of July, instant attraction. You wanted me bad."

I raised an eyebrow at him. "Did I?"

Last night had been that. And much more. It was comfort and caring. It was...I'm not sure what it was, but it was more than sex.

"'Moon River' playing in the background?" I teased.

"More like 'Hot in Herre'."

I rolled my eyes. This conversation was more than about Saturday night. I suspected it was his way of lightening what we'd experienced last night.

It wouldn't work. I remembered this one. But I appreciated the effort. He didn't want us to feel awkward. We couldn't let any feelings that might be developing between us get in the way of what we had to do.

"I can't believe you've forgotten. You practically jumped my bones right there in the bar," he insisted.

He chomped on another bite of doughnut.

"Simon Talbot, you are full of—"

He flicked his towel at me. "Don't offend my delicate ears with your foul language."

"I was going to say 'it'."

But there was truth to what he was saying. The attraction between us was really strong. I'm sure we'd felt it Saturday as well. I couldn't remember the last time I'd been in the presence of a man who made my breath catch simply by walking into the same room I was in. And who could somehow make me feel safe at the same time.

Simon stretched and pulled a carton of milk from the fridge, and I realized something more. He was trying to distract me. For some reason he didn't want to tell me exactly what had happened at the bar.

Or after we'd gotten back to his house.

Why? Surely it was more than his male ego.

"I don't pick up strange men," I stated evenly.

"Neither do I. Or strange women."

"Then why did I come home with you?"

"I invited you back to see my living room art. Not exactly etchings, but you seemed interested anyway."

I looked at him and tried to recreate in my mind what must have happened. I had been arguing with Wes. Simon interrupted and told me he was Michael's brother. How would I have reacted? I would have been skeptical. So I would have asked him for some I.D. He most likely had shown me his badge and maybe his driver's license and then given me the story of his mother's two marriages. I would have been intrigued that I'd missed him in my research and planned to check out his story. But I had gone home with him anyway. Why?

He had to have shown me something or enticed me in some way with more than his obvious sex appeal. But he hadn't wanted to share whatever it was with Wes. So somehow he'd managed to steal a moment alone with me and...what?

"I know you showed me your living room when we got back here Saturday night." Seeing it would have opened lots of emotions. I would have recognized him for what he was—one of the survivors, who, like me, was so caught up in what had happened fifteen years ago that it still dominated his life. And that was why I had trusted him, just as I trusted the others.

"But you told me you had something else for me to see—before we left the bar. What was it?" I asked.

He looked surprised. "Something you probably don't want to see right now."

"Show me."

He didn't argue. Instead he disappeared into the living room and came back with a bulky folder that he flopped down on top of Al's papers. I opened it. It was photocopies of Luther Isaacs' psychiatric reports from prison.

"How'd you get this?" I demanded.

"I can't tell you."

"Can't or won't?"

"Won't will do. Read it."

He walked out and I lost myself in the pages.

Chapter 10

"Isaacs' prison psychiatrists found no evidence of psychopathic behavior. What kind of quacks do they have—"

"Very good quacks with excellent credentials," Simon assured me.

He'd left me alone long enough to read the entire file. Then he'd come back into the kitchen, this time with his shirt on and clean shaven, looking as though he were ready for the day.

But Simon, at that moment, was the last thing on my mind. I was truly shaken.

"Maybe Isaacs is so good he fooled his doctors," I suggested. "There have been some cases where inmates actually convinced their psychiatrists they had various conditions such as multiple personalities when it was nothing but play acting. Psychopaths are charmers. Some of them seem totally normal."

Again that strange look from Simon as though he were experiencing déjà vu. Was I so stubborn that I always said the same thing in any particular situation?

"And maybe he didn't fool anyone," he said. Simon's playfulness was all gone. In its place was the determination I was familiar with. "Maybe Isaacs had another motive the night of the murders, other than a killing spree. Maybe one of the eight was his intended victim, and the other deaths were only to confuse the issue. Maybe Isaacs is a clever murderer, but no psychopath."

I couldn't help but feel he was easing me into some kind of theory he'd formed. He didn't believe Isaacs was the killer, so why was he saying he might be? So I would listen to him? I met his gaze.

"You're playing with semantics. No normal person would kill seven innocent people to disguise one murder."

The thought made my stomach churn. It was almost easier to take if they'd all been random instead of some kind of twisted window dressing.

"Besides, you don't think Isaacs was the killer," I added.

"Fine. Let's take Isaacs completely out of the equation," he suggested. "We could have a single intended victim among the dead. Don't tell me you've never thought about that."

I had. Many nights. In my nightmares, I'd even wondered if I might have been the one. But I knew I wasn't. Isaacs' car would have stopped. He would have come back and shot me, standing there stunned on the sidewalk, young, naive, exposed, unable to run—before I'd crumpled to the ground and pulled David's head into my lap to watch helplessly as he died. If Isaacs had wanted me dead, I would have been dead that night. And if anyone was an intended victim, it wasn't David Harrison. The shooter had been content to have either one of us. Because David had taken one step to the left, he was the one.

"Who do you think it might have been?" I asked.

"I couldn't find a link between Isaacs and any of the victims, short of maybe shopping at the same grocery store. That's one of the reasons I doubt he did it."

"If you think there was a single intended victim among the lot, just tell me who you think it was," I insisted again.

He hesitated one moment too long. "I don't know who it might have been. I'm just saying it's a possibility. Any investigator as good as you are knows she has to be willing to discard a hypothesis when the facts she uncovers no longer fit her theory. If you want to live to finish your film, you need to open yourself to other ideas. You may have been wrong all these years, Eva. Luther Isaacs may not be your man."

My whole body went numb as the words Simon had been saying since I first met him finally took hold. My existence for the past fifteen years had been based on Luther Isaacs being the murderer of the August Eight. He had to be. He had to pay for what he did. David had died.

If Simon was right, how did I turn off the hatred that had taken all of my energy for so many years? How could I be objective about the one thought that had driven my entire adult life?

Yet I knew that everything that had been happening opened the possibility that someone else might be guilty. Isaacs was either stupid enough to start up the killings again, or his release had triggered someone else's rampage, timed to bring Isaacs back under suspicion.

"Are you all right? You're pale."

I felt Simon touch my arm and looked up to see him staring at me, worry lines again at the sides of his eyes.

"I saw Isaacs' car the night of the murders."

"You saw a Ford Fairmont—"

"I saw *Luther Isaacs' car*. The image of it—the color, the puttied place on the fender, the pine tree air freshener swinging from the rear view mirror—is burned in my memory. When that bullet hit David, the world stopped as I memorized every detail. I don't care if they said my testimony wasn't enough. Isaacs might not have been driving it, but it *was* his car."

"But if you saw all of that, why *didn't* you see who was in the car?"

I could feel the frustration welling up inside me just as it had when the police had questioned me.

"It was night and the inside of the car was dark. The light from the street lamp didn't reach that far inside. The person driving was all the way across the seat from me. I'm telling you all that I remember. Don't you think that if I were embellishing any of the details, I *would* have described the driver?"

"Okay. I believe you. It was Isaacs' car."

I still wasn't ready to let go of the idea that Isaacs was the shooter. "The reports say Isaacs was a model prisoner. He never caused any trouble, but that means nothing."

"The police couldn't link him to the shootings, only to the stolen merchandise. If they'd been able to, he would have been prosecuted. We need to look beyond Isaacs. I don't think he's the one who tried to run you off the road last night."

I thought about the incident on the George Washington Parkway. Did I really believe a man who had been incarcerated for fifteen years, a man who was now in his fifties and who hadn't been behind the wheel of a car all that time was actually capable of that type of driving?

Maybe. Honest answer? No.

"He could still have done the original murders. What if Isaacs used an accomplice?" I suggested.

"Fifteen years ago?"

"Maybe, but not necessarily."

His voice softened as he leaned against the wall, relaxing his stance. "But now? Okay, let's go with that."

I had the uneasy feeling Simon was still leading me along, trying to shape my thoughts. But I played along anyway. "And this accomplice, if he were somehow in on the original murders, has been lying low all this time?"

"Probably not. If he was involved with Isaacs, he would have adopted a different modus operandi from what the two of them followed, but he would have continued his killing—if he were able to do it by himself."

As Simon said the words, I still doubted there'd been more than one murderer that night. There'd been only one shadow in the car. And in all of my investigations of Luther Isaacs, I'd never found any hint of an accomplice.

But now might be different. Christopher. Neither of us said his name, but he'd met with his father several times. They were blood related. Who knew what twisted thoughts a son who had a murderer for a father might grow up with.

"I'm just saying, it may have been someone else," Simon insisted. "Keep an open mind."

I'd try but every fiber within me was resisting.

"If not Isaacs, then who?"

Simon shrugged. "Think about the personalities. Who among the families and friends might be unbalanced enough to kill someone in this manner and to start up the killings years later?"

"No one," I insisted. We had our share of messed up kids. Claire's niece was a good example. So was Karen Durwood's son. Maybe Wes. And there were others. Some people would have added my own name to that list.

"You know how hard losing someone to murder can be. At least you were older. Try coping with something like that when you're in your teens or younger."

"That's my point," he said softly.

"Stop it!" I covered my ears with my hands.

"I thought you wanted the truth," Simon insisted quietly, standing up straight.

I dropped my hands, ashamed for my outburst, but not ashamed of my feelings. We'd all been through enough. It was overwhelming to have someone accuse a family member, who'd suffered so much, of killing someone he or she loved. But I hadn't known these people before the murders. I couldn't vouch for either their sanity or their stability.

"I do want the truth," I said. "But I don't want wild speculation about people who were every bit as much victims as the people who died.

"If I hadn't been with David when he died, would you be suspicious of me?" I spat out.

"I might," he said gently.

"You weren't with your brother. Why shouldn't I suspect that *you* wanted *him* dead."

"You should. But I wasn't even in the state at the time."

"Can you prove that?"

"Do I need to?"

When I didn't answer, he leaned back against the wall as though I'd never been angry.

"I stopped back by to see Wilma after I left your house yesterday," Simon said. "I thought she could use some help getting Al's car out of impound."

Al drove a silver-blue Chevy, the most nondescript car I'd ever seen. It was so generic in appearance I couldn't have told anyone the model or the year. Perfect for a private eye.

"The detectives investigating Al's homicide really didn't know it was there?"

"Nope. Wilma was exactly right. Classic case of the right hand not knowing what the left hand was doing. And Wilma wasn't about to tell them—not until she'd had a chance to go through it."

"Find anything?"

Simon's slow smile returned. "A few of his notes were there."

"Why didn't you mention this earlier when we were talking about Al's notes?"

I wondered what else Simon might have neglected to share with me.

"I could have but there wasn't much new to tell you. And I didn't think you were open then to what I'm about to say. Isaacs called a cab when he took off Sunday evening. Al followed him to the bar in Dupont Circle where we'd met Saturday evening, arriving about nine P.M."

"A cab? That means Isaacs left a paper trail. Why would he do that if he intended to harm either me or Wes? Surely he wouldn't have been that careless."

"Who says he was. He was meeting you in a public place. I doubt that he wanted anything more than to talk to you, at least not that night."

"And you don't have any other notes?"

"Not from the car. Anything else he would have written down must have been on him. Al obviously got out to pursue Isaacs on foot."

"Why obviously?" It was my turn to lean forward.

"There was no blood in Al's car."

So Al was killed elsewhere and then transported to my house in some other vehicle. He'd been wrapped in a garbage bag, which indicated preplanning on someone's part, but my money was on trace evidence being left in the transport vehicle, if we only knew which one and where it was. My mind was racing.

"Isaacs had no car," I said.

"Right. And the murderer didn't use Al's."

"A fourth person must have showed up Sunday night. Maybe Isaacs' accomplice," I suggested.

"Maybe."

"The police found nothing on Al's body—no notes, no papers, no weapons," I repeated.

"Right. Not even an I.D. Someone went through his pockets. Wilma wants you to come by. She has something she needs to talk to you about."

"What?"

"I don't know. She wouldn't tell me. Seems she still thinks of you as her client."

Actually, her partner.

I ran upstairs and threw on some jeans and a shirt. I was back downstairs in five minutes, pulling on my jacket. I stopped short. No Jeep.

"I'll be glad to give you a ride," Simon offered.

He was already at the front door before I called out. "Don't bother. I'll take the Honda."

"You sure?"

"Positive."

If Wilma hadn't told Simon what she wanted to tell me,

she didn't want him to know it. And at this point, I had to trust her judgment.

"When will you be back?"

"I don't know. Maybe five," I guessed, as I pulled on my gloves and wondered why Simon needed to know. Then I opened the backdoor.

"What? No good-bye kiss?"

I blushed. Before I could answer, he was at my side and I was in his arms. His kiss tingled on my lips as I went down the porch stairs.

"Don't forget me while you're gone," he called after me.

Chapter 11

"Tea?" Wilma offered, from behind Al's large, oak desk which was every bit as messy it had been when Al used it. She'd never gotten down the whole coffee and cigarettes routine more appropriate for a private eye. A lingering odor did, however, make me suspect she occasionally smoked cigars.

I shook my head as I took the old office chair with the green vinyl seat that she offered me. Tea was too civilized a drink for me, even if she did choose to drink hers out of a Starbucks travel mug.

"Simon told me he came by and helped you with Al's car."

"He's a good man," she offered. "I didn't want my daughter to have to go down there and get their father's car out of hock, especially when I didn't know what we might find, but I needed a second person to drive my car back for me." She took a deep breath. "Simon and I looked through it before I called homicide to let them know it had been located."

"I take it you conveniently forgot to tell the police about finding his notes."

"Did I? At my age it's really hard to remember every little detail that someone might want to know. I'm sure they've got it all cleaned out by now, better than having it detailed. Can you imagine? They'll test every one of those greasy food wrappers and cigarette butts. Personally, I think they should save their money. My money says whoever killed Al was never anywhere near his car."

I leaned forward in my chair. "Simon said you wanted to talk to me."

"There were three notes in your file," she said, opening a manila folder lying on her desk and glancing over the top page. "It says here you left a message on Al's phone sometime Saturday evening saying that you were going home with Simon Talbot. You asked Al to check him out."

I already knew I'd gone home with Simon, but I didn't know I'd alerted Al. I must have slipped away from the table and made the call from the restroom.

"My, my, my," she added with a tsk, tsk, tsk.

I blushed. "It wasn't like that, Wilma," I lied. "This was business. Simon had some information he needed to show me."

"Pity."

The disapproving matronly expression Wilma had adopted disappeared and the corners of her eyes lifted. "I'm not judging you, sweetie. A man like that doesn't come along just any day."

Wilma might like Simon, but Al wouldn't have been won over so easily.

"I have a note here that Al called you back."

I could only imagine the lecture he'd started to give me and how I'd cut him off.

"He made several phone calls from his car that night," she went on, "and did some Internet searches. He did confirm that Simon is currently with the Pittsburgh P.D., has been for the last twelve years, and that his colleagues speak very highly of him. He's been at his current address for one month. He's on leave from the department. His current means of support is not readily evident. I'm assuming Al told you all of this. He has a note here that he returned your call late Saturday evening."

I nodded. I had no idea what Al had told me, but everything Wilma was saying agreed with what Simon had told me. Whatever information Al had given me must have been enough to make me comfortable with staying with

Simon. Part of me may have remembered that it was okay to go with him when we'd left together yesterday morning. I'd put it down to instinct, but it might have been more. And, of course, there was the revelation that he was one of us, one of the victims' family members.

"That may have been all the research he had time for before we lost him." Wilma swallowed hard, but her voice didn't change. "If there was more, I don't have it. His phone was never recovered. Did he call you Sunday?"

I shook my head. If he did, I had no memory of it.

"You said there were three notes."

"I'm getting to the others." She took a big sip of tea. I recognized the aroma of Constant Comment—and something else. Was that bourbon I smelled mixed in with her tea? It made me wonder what this woman was doing in this business when she should have been reading to her grandchildren.

"Al was fascinated by psychopaths, about the same as you. You didn't ask for it, but he did some more digging into Isaacs' past."

I'd done my own digging as well. I knew there was no evidence that Isaacs had demonstrated true psychopathic tendencies, but I'd held fast to the belief that didn't mean he didn't have them. Tortured animals often go unrecorded, as do familial abuse, solitary tendencies, and fetish behavior. Just because there was no record didn't make it not so.

Wilma tapped her finger on the folder as though considering how I might react to what she was about to say. "When Isaacs was in basic training, he saved a man's life."

First Simon, and now Wilma. I didn't move a muscle.

"He pulled a man out of the deep end of the pool during an endurance exercise. The man had gone into an asthmatic attack. I just thought you ought to know."

"What else you got?"

I didn't want to be dismissive, but that account proved nothing. Performance before a group, altruistic or otherwise, was also not out of character for a psychopath. And, murderer or not, the man was no saint. He was a convicted thief. He could have dived into that pool for the praise and the attention, not to save the man's life.

Wilma narrowed her eyes. "If you've got your gun trained in only one direction, it's easy for someone to sneak up behind you."

"I know Isaacs may not have been the killer, and that he may not be behind the current attacks."

There. I'd said it out loud.

"Good. That makes you safer already."

She took a deep breath, and I knew she'd saved what she really wanted me to hear for last.

"You know the name Carolyn Akers?"

I placed my arm on the desk to steady myself. She was the other witness who had seen Isaacs' car that night. She'd died in a freak, one-car accident two days after the shootings.

"What about her?"

"Al was looking into her death."

I stared hard at Wilma, my heart speeding a little faster in my chest. Carolyn had died while Isaacs was in custody.

"That death was an accident. The police investigated it at the time and found no evidence of foul play."

"No evidence means no evidence. It doesn't mean it didn't occur."

She didn't need to remind me of that. When it had happened, I'd been so sure someone had murdered Carolyn, I'd freaked out my parents. I'd slept with the light on for over a month and a baseball bat lying next to me in my bed. Carolyn and I had been the only two to see that car.

Jesse had assured both me and my parents that I was safe—that the police had their man—but I wouldn't be comforted. He'd even put an officer on detail to watch my house for a week until I settled down.

But what if Carolyn had seen more than I had? She'd

lived across the street from the Durwood house. There was talk she might have caught a brief glimpse of the driver. What if she could have identified Isaacs?

What if she could have cleared him?

I swallowed. "What did Al have on it?"

"He'd gotten hold of the photos taken at the scene of the accident. There were no skid marks on the pavement. It happened about two in the morning. She was with a friend. They'd both been drinking, and they were coming back from a club downtown. They went off the road and plunged into the Potomac."

I knew all the details. She could have walked out into four lanes of traffic with twenty witnesses watching her every move, and, at the time, I still would have been convinced Isaacs had somehow manipulated her death on a busy highway. That's how paranoid I'd been. But the police had assured us it was an accident. They had their man and no one would be coming after me. They'd been right.

Until now.

I closed my eyes. Carolyn had just celebrated her thirtieth birthday the month before she'd died. I'd already outlived her by two years.

"Was he able to get a copy of Carolyn's statements to the police?"

"Yes, but they were preliminary. She wasn't able to give a good description, certainly not as accurate as the one you'd given of the car. They planned to work with her some more, bring in a hypnotist—"

"But they didn't get the chance."

She might not have seen the murderer well, but he'd seen her. And he'd known where she lived. Right across the street from one of the victims.

"Al took copies of the photos of the wreckage to a friend to be enhanced. He was looking for a sign of paint from another vehicle anywhere on the car. I haven't gotten the report back yet." She studied my face. "I don't think we'll find anything."

The fact that Al thought we might meant he was convinced Carolyn had been murdered. Which meant he believed Isaacs was innocent.

I was stunned, but Wilma didn't seem to notice.

"I'll keep digging," she assured me.

"I never doubted you would."

She gave me a look. "We won't get anything that could ever be used in court."

"I know."

I stood up, my legs a lot less steady than they'd been when I came in, and gave Wilma a hug across her desk.

Whatever the truth was, the murders of the August Eight were shaping up into much more than one thrill kill spree on a summer night.

When I left Wilma's, I took a few moments in the parking lot to make some calls.

I spoke briefly with Claire who assured me she was doing much better, that the doctors expected to release her probably tomorrow. She, true to character, was far more interested in how I was holding up. It was good to hear her voice. And I was glad she was someplace safe, at least for the moment.

I'd sworn to keep to my filming schedule, but neither Debra Roddy nor Ben needed to be near me when I was a target. I called Ben and told him I was canceling the second interview at Debra's home scheduled for that afternoon. I also called Debra and made certain she'd heard about the shootings. She assured me she'd be careful, but she wasn't going to give up the life she'd worked so hard to build. I couldn't blame her for that. Her grandmother would have been proud of her.

Chapter 12

I got back to Simon's a lot earlier than I'd expected with a peace offering of lunch in my saddlebag, anxious to see him. He'd done nothing except try to help me since I'd met him, and I'd been pretty hard on him about Isaacs. It seemed that everyone—Al, Wilma, and Simon—refused to convict Isaacs without more evidence. The least I could do was listen with a more open mind.

As I pulled around to the back of the house, I saw a dark, beat-up sedan parked close to the porch. The pace of my heart quickened. The car belonged to Christopher Isaacs.

How could he have found us?

I drew off my gloves and helmet, grasped my gun, and silently cursed. I held steady for a moment, weighing the situation as the motor idled on my Honda. The noise from my bike would have announced my arrival. I'd already lost any element of surprise I'd like to have had.

Even if Christopher wasn't behind the current shootings, he'd just compromised the one place I'd felt safe. He could easily tell his father where I was. I didn't want Isaacs anywhere near me. Even if he did prove to be innocent, I doubted I would ever be comfortable around him. And I knew a part of Christopher had to hate me, as well. He had to know I'd spoken against his father at every one of his parole hearing.

I was a lot more angry than frightened. If Christopher had tried something, I was confident he'd be no match for Simon. The photo Al had taken of him showed a scrawny kid. Besides, if he'd meant either of us harm, surely he would have come at night and parked elsewhere, so he could sneak up on us undetected.

So what the hell *did* he want?

Maybe what he wanted didn't matter. Maybe he could be of value to Simon and me—if indeed he wasn't the one who'd shot at me and Claire. It hadn't been his car on the George Washington Parkway. I also wondered how adept Christopher was at stealing cars.

I cut the engine, left my helmet hanging from the handle bars and climbed off the bike. Then I headed up the stairs to the porch, lunch in my left hand, my right hand gripping the pistol in the pocket of my jacket.

"Anyone for steak burritos?" I announced as the door clanged shut behind me.

"Christopher, I want you to meet—" Simon began.

"I know who she is," Christopher interrupted.

He made a swift movement, and I wrapped my index finger around the trigger. But he simply held out his empty hand for me to shake.

I looked quickly in Simon's direction. He seemed relaxed, and gave me a slight nod.

I let go of the pistol, drew my hand out of my pocket, and shook Christopher's hand. He obviously read the distrust in my face, quickly reclaiming his hand and stuffing it into his front jeans pocket which was too shallow to be hiding any weapons. He had on a long-sleeved blue T-shirt with navy bands around the neck and both sleeves and a band logo printed across his chest in red.

"You must think me showing up here is weird."

"That's an understatement," I admitted.

He gave me an easy smile. "I know you're looking into the August Eight killings. You're going to clear my dad. You don't believe that right now, but you are. You're fair. I've seen all of your work. You'll dig and you'll find it out, like you did in the Esteban case."

The Esteban murder spree was a bizarre farmhouse

blood bath out in the middle of nowhere in far western Maryland. The conviction of a neighbor boy was a slam dunk for the police. But as I did the interviews for my documentary, I'd become suspicious of another neighbor. It turned out he had the murder weapon buried in his back yard.

I studied Christopher. He seemed innocuous and even younger than he actually was. And Simon had let him in.

Or had he invited him in? How *had* Christopher found Simon's house? I'd have to ask Simon later.

We ate the burritos as we talked, standing around in the kitchen, sauce dripping into the wrappers the food had come in. I watched Christopher as he chatted, looking for something in his body language to give him away, to let me know he was other than he seemed, but I found nothing. He was still lanky and moved liked a teenager, and he had a naive attitude that insisted that someday, somehow all would be right with the world. I wondered where he'd gotten it. Not from his father, and certainly not from his mother. Perhaps his Aunt Mary Ann.

He refused Simon's offer of beer, instead going outside and bringing in the Coke he'd brought with him in his car.

"You've visited with your father since he was released from prison," I said casually, as I wadded up the wrappers from our food and tossed them into the trash.

He cocked his head, but didn't ask how I knew. "Dad was staying with my aunt Mary Ann. She liked having me come by."

"But your mom didn't like it," Simon added.

"Nope." Christopher offered a forced grin. "My mom doesn't like much of anything, and nothing that has to do with my dad."

"Where is he now?" I asked. That question was getting old.

"I don't know." Suddenly, he looked his age, maybe even older. "I've been waiting for him to call, but he hasn't.

Even if he does, he won't tell me, not with the police looking for him. I know you were watching him. I spotted the guy you had on him when I visited him. You're looking for the wrong man. That's why I came here. I want you to let me help find out who's really behind the shootings."

I believed him. I also believed that if he wanted to do us harm, he would have tried something by now. I'd kept on my jacket. My gun was in my pocket, and I had no doubt Simon was also armed.

"The man you spotted is dead," I said evenly.

If he was surprised, he didn't show it. He'd probably recognized Al's photo on the television news reports.

"My dad didn't shoot him, and he didn't shoot at you," Christopher said. No frills, no steel to his words, a simple statement of fact.

"How can you be so sure?" I asked. If Christopher were the one behind the recent shootings, he'd know for sure his father was innocent.

He didn't answer. He simply laid a piece of paper on the counter by the sink. I had no doubt he'd been defending his father all his life, and nobody had listened.

"Here's my phone number and my address. Call me when you decide to let me help."

I picked up the paper and shoved it into my jeans pocket.

Then he left without another word. We listened to his car crank and then leave the driveway.

"You let him in," I accused.

Simon looked straight into my eyes. "You would have, too. Besides, it's my house."

It was. And I had no right to tell Simon how to manage the situation. But it made me uneasy knowing anybody, other than Simon, knew where I slept at night. Maybe that was why I was being testy with Simon.

"How'd he find us?"

"He didn't say."

"Surely he couldn't have followed us."

"I don't know. I don't think the kid's dangerous," Simon stated again.

I could feel my anger rising. "Oh, so everybody who loved someone who died with the August Eight is a suspect, but Isaacs' own son isn't?"

"He was a child when the murders occurred."

"Right. Well, he's no longer a child, Simon. And I bet he's a whole lot sharper than that easy going manner of his would suggest. He found us."

"He did indeed. Could he be behind what's going on now? Yes, but I don't see it."

"And what are you basing that on? Your cop's instinct?"

"I was right about you, wasn't I?"

"So you don't think I'm dangerous."

"Oh, I know you're dangerous. That's what makes you so much fun."

He came toward me, pulled me roughly to him, and kissed me hard on the mouth. I gave in to the kiss, enjoying the rush of pleasure that surged through me and the feel of his body against mine. Then I pushed him away, because I didn't need Simon distracting me when I had more to say. Not, at least, until later.

"Stay over there," I warned him, "and listen to me. I talked to Wilma. Al was looking into Carolyn Akers' death," I said.

His playful smile disappeared. "The other witness."

"He thought she was murdered."

"Did you ever doubt it?" A hint of condescension clouded his features, irritating the hell out of me. Why was he so certain? How much did Simon really know?

And why did he refuse to tell me?

"I tried to doubt it," I said, lifting my chin. "The police

told me they had the murderer in custody. I believed what I needed to finally close my eyes at night."

"Hey, it's all right," Simon soothed, again taking me in his arms, but gently this time. I let him, but I was convinced that nothing he could do or say was going to make me feel better.

I hadn't thought about Carolyn for many years. I couldn't afford to. I couldn't help but think I could have been dead as easily as she was. Isaacs' car had been in the farther lane, across from her side of the street. That put the driver closer to the window where the light could have picked up his features. She could have gotten a better look at whoever was behind the wheel that night.

If David and I had been walking on the other side of the street, would it have been my car that would have mysteriously gone into the Potomac?

Simon must have felt me shudder in his arms.

"*You* didn't die," he whispered in my ear. "Do you think things happen for a reason?"

"No." I knew they didn't. No one could convince me there was any reason for anyone to die that night.

"Well, I disagree."

Simon cupped my face in his hands so I had to look at him. "I think you were spared by whatever force, so that you could find out who did this and finally bring them to justice. And so..."

"And so what?"

He let go of my face and again wrapped his arms around me so tightly I couldn't get away. "And so you and I could have crazy, wild sex."

He made me laugh. And that was exactly what I needed.

Simon had gone out and the bar in Dupont Circle wouldn't open for several hours. So I spent the rest of the afternoon with my feet up on Simon's lumpy couch immersed in the letters Mary Ann had given me that Isaacs had written to her from prison. I hoped that if, indeed, Isaacs had been framed as Simon suggested he might have, there would be something in his writings that might point to who could have done it.

The letters ran the gamut from confusion, self pity, and self loathing to resignation and finally spiritual redemption. I rolled my eyes. The sinner who had found God was a little too cliché. And if Isaacs really was the innocent with a new belief in God, then where the hell was he? Why wasn't he seeking us out to enlist our help in proving his innocence?

Or had he done just that? Is that why he'd wanted to meet with me at the bar?

Throughout Isaacs' letters was what appeared to be a genuine concern for Christopher, both how he was coping with his father being in prison and how he could find a moral life, especially when Isaacs' ex-wife was crazy as a loon. He'd put much of that burden on Mary Ann.

What I wasn't reading in the letters was arrogance or egomania. Indeed, Isaacs seemed more and more humbled as the letters progressed.

Isaacs was a thief and an alcoholic who occasionally used drugs. A sinner. He freely admitted it over and over. But he insisted over and over again, he hadn't stolen the goods found in the trunk of his car. Yet his fingerprints had been on them.

As for murder, he remained, throughout the entire fifteen years, insistent that he could not, would not, ever murder anyone. He said that he had been tested and, by the grace of God, he had passed that test. He would never take a human life. Murder was wrong. He believed in the fires of damnation.

I wasn't at all sure I believed in them, but I had often pictured him being consumed by them.

I wondered how Isaacs could be so sure what he'd *not* done that night, considering the condition he'd been in when the cops had arrested him.

He'd been in and out of jail many times. He'd served eighteen months for one offense, two years for another. Apparently he was well known by the police.

He mentioned Jesse by name as having arrested him twice and as having taken him home from a bar when his conduct had become somewhat disorderly. Jesse did things like that. But he'd told me once, it wasn't always out of compassion. He said to combat your enemy on the street, you had to get to know him.

Isaacs was self-admittedly one of the bad guys. So what made *this* theft different? How could he expect anyone to believe his pleas of innocence?

The answer I found in the letters was that he didn't care whether or not anyone did—except for his son, Christopher.

And Christopher had made it clear that his father had succeeded. Unless Christopher was trying to deceive us. No. My instincts were saying the same thing that Simon's were: the kid was sincere.

But that didn't mean his father was. It only meant he'd managed to convince his son.

I had to remind myself that if Isaacs hadn't committed the original killings, he could still be behind the current shootings. He'd had fifteen years of his life taken from him. He could blame the families, those of us who were so intent on putting him away. He could well have shot at me and injured Claire. He might now be exacting his vengeance. I couldn't afford to let my guard down around the son, not if there was any possibility that he was in league with his father.

I went into the kitchen, poured myself another cup of coffee, and took it back with me to the couch. Unfortunately, we were out of doughnuts. I hoped Simon remembered to buy some when he was at the grocery store.

I thought about doughnuts and I thought about Isaacs and the theft of the electronics found in his car. Doughnuts were a quick sugar fix, energy straight to the system, like a thief with a drug problem mugging somebody on the street for a twenty: it didn't solve the problem, but it made you feel like it did, at least for a little while.

Isaacs was a doughnut man. He held up convenience stores. He didn't break into stores after hours and steal upscale electronics. That required a fence or at least a pawn shop. Which was one more step before he got the money. It wasn't his MO. He was always a little too desperate for that next bottle of booze or that next high. He wasn't the sort to devise an elaborate plan, and, from what I could tell, he had no one to suggest one to him. It made me wonder.

What if Mary Ann was right? What if Isaacs hadn't stolen those electronics?

Simon and the psychiatrists at the prison had opened my mind to the possibility of Isaacs' innocence. The letters supported that theory. But if he had been framed, why him? Was he merely a convenient patsy or was there something else?

"You still reading those letters?"

Simon startled me as he spoke from the doorway into the kitchen. My hand instinctively folded over the gun lying next to my piles of paper before I realized what I was doing. I hadn't heard his key in the lock or the back door open.

"Actually I'm about finished for now. Did you bring me something good?"

"No more doughnuts, if that's what you were hoping for. Steak, potatoes, a bag of salad, and a bottle of wine."

"And for dessert?"

"There's always me."

I grinned. "That'll more than do."

I was really looking forward to my first home-cooked meal in ages. And what would follow it.

I glanced at my watch. It was almost five o'clock.

"When do we eat?" I asked.

"I was thinking seven-thirty."

"I'm assuming you're doing the cooking because we're in trouble if you think I know how to turn on a stove."

"If you call broiling cooking."

"Perfect."

I grabbed my jacket and slipped it on.

"You going out?" he asked. He seemed disappointed.

I went over to him and gave him a peck on the cheek like we'd been married ten years.

We hadn't. He pulled me to him and kissed me full on the lips, bringing my whole body alive. I drew back.

"Later, babe," I promised.

He let me go, but he grabbed hold of the thin cylinder of black metal that I kept on a chain snapped on the side of the breast pocket of my jacket.

"I've been meaning to ask you what this is," he said.

"It's a kubotan."

He raised an eyebrow.

"Barry gave it to me. It's used in martial arts. When it's forcefully applied to some of the pressure points of the body, it can take a man down. I feel better having it where I can get to it if I need it, like the pepper spray on my key ring."

"I don't suppose you'd like to give me a demonstration."

"Believe me, you wouldn't enjoy it."

"I know what I would enjoy," he said, kissing me again.

My head swam and for half a moment I forgot why I needed to leave. I had no time for what we both wanted to do.

"I'm out of here, but I won't be long," I promised, shoving him away. "I like steak."

"That's not all you like. I'll be waiting for you when you get back."

Chapter 13

Happy hour at a D.C. bar is chaos. Cheap drinks and free snacks. Some of the people at Dupont Circle had been waiting all day for the opportunity to relax with their coworkers. They crowded into the narrow storefront like heathens awaiting salvation.

It was dark inside, with wood paneling running down the side with the bar and a brick wall opposite it. Ten to fifteen small tables lined one after the other made maneuvering almost impossible, but I managed to make my way to the far end of the bar.

I waited for a gal who was into her third martini to finish and swiped her stool as she headed for the restroom.

"What'll you have?" the bartender asked. He was tall and husky and somebody you wouldn't want to mess with. My guess was he did double duty as the bouncer.

I'd watched him as I'd waited. He kept close tabs on his patrons. That's how he made his tips. And how he made sure nobody went over their limit.

"Were you working this weekend?" I asked.

"If you don't work in this business, you don't get paid," he told me with a smile.

I nodded. "Saturday night I was in here. Do you remember seeing me?"

"Right over there."

He pointed to a small, round table well away from the door and currently overflowing with three women and one man.

"I was with someone."

"You drinking while we talk?"

"Absolutely. I'll have a beer."

He disappeared before I could tell him what kind. When he came back he set a glass and an opened bottle of Dos Equis in front of me. I was impressed.

"Could you describe the people I was with?"

He gave me a peculiar look, and I dropped two twenties in his tip jar.

"A thin, good-looking, dark-haired guy who seemed agitated. Another dark-haired guy who looked to be a little older and like he was into lifting weights joined the two of you. He'd been sitting at the bar watching you. He seemed pretty into you. Is this some kind of test?"

"You might say that."

So he'd seen me with Wes and he'd seen Simon join us.

"Who came in first? Me or the guy at the bar?"

"You. The guy at the bar followed about a minute or two later."

"Anyone else?"

"Nope." His brow knitted as his eyes narrowed. "Just you and the two guys."

"Can you tell me what happened?"

"I thought they were going to get into a shoving match and that I might have to come over there, but you handled them."

"I left with the older guy?"

"Yeah. I could have predicted that from the get-go."

I tried to control the color I could feel rising in my cheeks.

"And the younger guy?"

"He left a few minutes later."

"And Sunday night?"

"You were here with the younger guy again. He was waiting for you and you joined him, although you weren't real happy with him. But then you hadn't been Saturday night either."

"Were we arguing?"

"Not loudly, but you were not pleased. Neither was he. About fifteen minutes later another dude showed up. White hair. Flabby. Looked like he'd been around the block one too many times."

Isaacs.

"Did you see another middle-aged guy with a beard come in about the same time as the white-haired man? He would have been wearing a brown windbreaker and khaki pants."

"Yeah. Him, I wouldn't normally remember, but he ordered a shot of Dalwhinnie with water on the side. Don't get much call for that in here. He sat at the end of the bar near the door. Was he with you because he sure didn't seem to be?"

I shook my head. Al was good.

"Did we leave together?"

"Yeah, you, the young guy, and the white-haired man. About 11:30."

"And the guy at the bar?"

"I'm not sure, but it must have been about the same time as you. I found the scotch, untouched on the bar. Left three bills under the glass."

"Thanks," I told him, dropping several bills on the counter for the beer. "I don't suppose you heard any kind of disturbance, maybe something that sounded like a car backfiring that night?"

He shook his head and then put a hand on my arm as I got up to leave.

"You in some kind of trouble?" he asked.

"Always," I assured him.

Outside the air was brisk. A man and two women broke from the pack of walkers crowding the sidewalk and pushed past me into the bar, as traffic clipped along the street.

Late Sunday night would have been less crowded, but parking was always difficult, even on a weekend.

I stepped back against the storefront, pulled a small street map from my pocket, and unfolded it to get my bearings. Al had parked one street over, at least that's where the tow ticket said his car had been found. That meant he'd had to waste precious time finding a place to park after Isaacs had been let off by the cab in front of the bar.

I'd marked the cross streets where the 7-Eleven was located. Two long blocks east and one block north. I started walking. I was assuming I'd gone on foot and not alone since Wes, Isaacs, and I had come out together. I'd had no vehicle, neither had Isaacs. Were we going to meet someone else? Had Isaacs wanted to show me something? Why had I left with him? I would have known better than to do that.

There was a fairly wide alley immediately to my right. I stepped into it and stopped, as a shiver ran up my spine. There had to have been a confrontation between the bar and the convenience store. Blood had been spilled. I'd gotten it on my hands. Where? It had to have been somewhere out of the public flow, otherwise someone would have called the police. But there were lots of alleys between here and the 7-Eleven where I'd wound up, lots of places where I might have hurt my head. Had someone struck me or had I fallen?

I'd been running that night. I remembered the feeling in my chest, the shortness of breath when I'd suddenly become aware of my surroundings. What had I been running from?

Had Isaacs killed Al and tried to kill Wes and me?

My head ached from so many questions and so few answers. I tried to think. Al's body had shown up at my house. But where the hell was Wes?

I let the thought that I'd been avoiding since early Monday morning fully form in my mind. The reason I hadn't heard from Wes might be because he was dead. The possibility sickened me. What I feared even more was why I couldn't remember. Had I somehow been responsible for both Al's and Wes's deaths? Could that be why I refused to remember?

Refused. The word brought me up short. Is that what was going on?

I pushed the thought away. Even if I were suffering from some sort of hysterical amnesia, subconsciously trying to protect myself, I had to know the truth. The key was to stay focused and not let the fear of what I might find out keep me from looking for the answers.

I stepped back onto the sidewalk and glanced again at the map. However I'd gotten to the 7-Eleven, I wouldn't be going through any alleys tonight, not by myself. I noted that the convenience store wasn't in the direction of Metro Center, so I hadn't been going to meet Simon.

I took off at a fast clip down the street, blending in with the pedestrians that filled the sidewalks, and noticing fewer and fewer people on the streets as I traveled east. I was drained by the time I got to the gas station. It looked different, not at all menacing as it had that night. I went inside.

"I'm looking for the man who does the after midnight shift in the booth outside," I explained to the Indian woman behind the counter, which was cluttered with candy and snacks. A hefty rack of cigarettes stood directly behind her.

"He's not here," she said.

"I realize that. Can you tell me where I can find him?"

She eyed me suspiciously, just as the other clerk had that night. "Why do you want to know?"

"I think I shorted him when I paid for my gasoline."

"No. He would have called the police, and I haven't had any police report."

"Look, if I leave a phone number for him to call, would you pass it along to—"

"You come back later. In two days. He'll be back on

shift then. After eleven o'clock. He'll be locked in his booth."

I nodded. I wasn't going to get more than that out of her and probably nothing from the night clerk as well.

I'd done all I could do downtown for now, and Simon would be expecting me for dinner. But first I needed to find someplace where I could sit down alone and think for a few minutes before I went back. He'd have questions for me, and I needed some answers to give him. How much did I dare trust Simon?

The steak was excellent. It was a relief to be back at Simon's and have him to distract my thoughts. He'd even scrounged up another chair so the two of us could sit properly at the table.

"What did you put on this?" I asked.

"A little mixture of my own," Simon said. "You like?"

"Oh, yes, I like very much."

His eyes met mine and I didn't think we were talking about steak anymore. I dropped my gaze back to the food.

"What'd you find out at the bar?"

"Not much. The bartender didn't see anyone else."

"No one lurking in the shadows?"

"That isn't funny, Simon."

He lost his smile. "You're right. It isn't. Why were you gone so long?"

"I walked the streets for a while after I left the bar, looking for anything familiar. Then I stopped in a café for coffee."

I'd wondered if every dark patch I'd passed on the sidewalk had been blood.

He watched me as I brooded, but he knew not to push. "You haven't touched your potato," was all he said.

"I'm getting there. It's delicious. Really. It's just that I don't have much of an appetite." But then I never did.

I attacked the spud. Simon had drenched it with butter

and sour cream. It was great having a man fix my food. Not one thought went to cholesterol or calories. I ate half of it before I laid down my fork.

"What am I missing here?" I asked.

"Did you want cheese or—"

I startled both him and myself by hitting the table with my palm, all of my frustrations finally welling up. Simon was looking at me as though I had two heads. I had to keep reminding myself that we'd just met. He didn't know my moods or that I had a temper that could flare without warning, especially when I was doing mundane, meaningless things like eating or laundry.

"How can we sit here and eat and talk like normal people?" I asked, trying to control the anger in my voice as I felt my chest heave. "I'm missing hours of my life. Hours. Anything could have happened, people could have been hurt, and I don't remember it."

I was again on the verge of tears, but I refused to cry.

"It'll come back," Simon promised calmly, his eyes assuring me he believed what he was saying.

"How could you know that?" I snapped.

"It almost always does within a few days, certainly less than a week."

"Even if it's psychological?"

"Especially if it's psychological. Brain injuries are a lot trickier. Sometimes the time loss comes back gradually. Sometimes it never comes back."

I was afraid of knowing what I'd blocked out—almost as much as I was afraid of not knowing. And I was disgusted with my cowardice.

"So now you're an expert on amnesia?" I asked, still lashing out.

"No. But I did some reading for a case we had in Pittsburgh a few years ago." His voice was calm, kind, soothing. He reached across the table and took my hand. Was that sincere compassion I read in his eyes?

"Within another day or so, you should remember everything."

I should have been reassured, but I wasn't. An unwelcome thought entered my mind. Was Simon waiting for my memory to come back? Could that be why he was with me, why he wanted to know where I was every minute, why he wanted me here in his home with him?

Last night and this morning I would have sworn that his motives were sincere. But as attracted as he might be to me, I sensed he was the sort of man who would see whatever mission he was on through to its conclusion. Just like me, he was here to find out who killed the August Eight. Could my memory hold the key?

"You need some rest," Simon said. "What say I dump these dishes in the sink and we go upstairs."

"For some rest?"

He smiled slyly. "Eventually."

Simon pulled me back into his embrace, his scent warm and inviting, as he gently kissed my nose, my cheeks, and finally my mouth again. We'd made love. I was taken in by the emotional draw of the man, a man who lived every day with some of the same wounds that I shared, wounds that had refused to heal for fifteen years.

His passion was strong, like Jackie's, mine, and Wes's. We all clung desperately to life, wanting to feel, to experience, wanting the cloud of uncertainty that enveloped us to finally go away, wanting to forget that we could die at any moment.

Or were those my issues that I was projecting onto Simon?

"You all right?" he asked, drawing back to look into my eyes.

I nodded, wanting to start all over again, to keep this moment for as long as possible so I could memorize every detail. So I could feel. So I didn't have to think.

I started to run my hand through his hair, but he immediately took hold of my wrist, gently bringing my hand to his lips for a kiss. Then he let go and abruptly got out of bed.

I sat up. "What's wrong?"

He was already pulling on his jeans and T shirt.

"Nothing." He kept his back to me while he tugged on his socks and his boots.

"Simon, what did I—"

"I just need some time alone."

And like that I was dismissed. He left the room as I sat there hugging the sheets to my chest, wondering what I could have done to make him leave, and why I refused to take a lover who wasn't emotionally scarred. I was one screwed up woman.

And Simon was one screwed up man.

I got dressed and went downstairs, but Simon wasn't there. I looked out the backdoor and saw that both the Mustang and our bikes were all still here. If he'd gone for a walk, he'd most likely be back soon. I hoped so. It was dark outside, and I didn't want to be alone tonight.

I closed the blinds and started washing the dishes. If he cooked, the least I could do was wash. And I needed something mindless to occupy my hands.

As I watched the suds bubble up over the plates and glasses I wondered what my life would have been like if David and I had gone to a movie that night in August instead of out for a walk. We would have come back to my parents' house, gone downstairs to the family room and probably watched television. A news bulletin would have interrupted the broadcast, and we would have watched, appalled at what had happened only a few blocks away from us. I would most likely have waited until the next day to break up with him over the phone.

Eventually the murders would have faded from my memory as they had for most of the public. Would I now be happily married? I'm sure David would be. Would I have children? Would cooking and washing dishes have been a nightly routine instead of an almost never event? How different would I have been? Would I feel safe when I closed my eyes at night?

I was still scrubbing the broiler with suds up to my elbows when Simon came back.

He dropped a box of doughnuts on the counter without a word, wrapped his arms around my waist, and kissed the back of my neck. It sent inviting shivers down my spine.

"Does this mean we're okay?" I asked, turning toward him and drying my hands on a paper towel.

"We always were," he insisted. But he headed back into the living room before I could return his embrace. I watched him go. I understood his need for space. Simon had secrets of his own. He wasn't upset with me. He was upset about them.

Before joining him, I decided to give Wes one more try. I dug my cell phone out of my bag and punched in his number. It rang only once before a man answered.

"Wes?"

"Evie?"

I couldn't believe what I was hearing. Tears stung my eyes. Thank God he was alive. But my relief immediately dissolved into anger. "Where the hell have you been? I've called and called—"

"Tell me you're not with that bastard Simon Talbot."

"Yes. How did you know I—"

"Crap. I was afraid of that. Can he hear us?"

Simon came back into the kitchen and stared at me with narrowed eyes. "Who are you talking to?"

"Hold on just a minute," I said into the mouthpiece.

I looked at Simon. I was afraid he might overhear our conversation and wondered why it would matter. He gave me a disapproving look.

I hesitated one minute too long. "I was just checking on Claire," I lied, surprised I felt it necessary not to tell Simon that Wes was on the line, especially when he knew I'd been trying to reach him.

"Is she all right?"

"She's better. I won't be long," I promised.

Simon seemed satisfied and his genuine concern made me feel horrible for lying to him. He went back into the living room, and I stepped outside onto the back porch.

"I was afraid you were dead," I said, lowering my voice.

"Not yet."

"Listen to me, Wes. I don't remember anything after leaving to meet you Saturday evening and nothing that happened Sunday."

"You shittin' me, Evie? Nothing? What happened to you?"

"I was hoping you could tell me that. Apparently I hurt my head."

"If you don't remember, how the hell did you hook back up with Talbot?"

"He had my Jeep. I don't really have time to explain right now. Wes, I've got to know—"

"Just listen before he gets wind of what's going on. Talbot's not playing straight with you. Don't believe a word that creep tells you."

"What are you talking about?... Wes?... Are you there?"

He coughed. "Yeah, I'm here. Don't turn your back on him. Get the hell out of there."

"Someone tried to kill me. And Claire—" I said.

"Tell me something I don't already know. Just listen. I've got a note from Al."

"How did you get—"

"Listen to me. I don't know how much time we've got.

Al had done some searching—why I don't know. Michael Whitehall never had a brother."

I felt the hair rise on the back of my neck as I forgot how to breathe. I turned and looked through the backdoor, thinking about the man inside that house who had sheltered me, fed me, who'd taken me into his bed.

"What are you saying?" I managed.

"I'm telling you Talbot isn't who he says he is. Whatever he's told you, Evie, is a lie. Get the hell out of there."

Chapter 14

I stared at the phone, wanting to heave it against the side of the house, hating Wes, cursing Simon, and remembering again why I could never truly trust anyone.

I didn't believe Wes. I *knew* not to believe him. But was I willing to bet my life that he was lying?

"Meet me in two hours at that little all night coffee shop in Bethesda where we used to go," Wes ordered.

"How did you get Al's notes?" I demanded once I again found my voice. But it was no use. Blood pounded in my temples as I stared at the phone, dead in my hand. I hit redial, thankful I didn't have to put in his phone number with the way my hand was shaking and cursing Wes for not telling me all that he knew. Seconds later I connected with Wes's voice mail. I slammed the phone off.

I didn't know what game Wes was playing—or what game Simon might be playing.

I again considered the man inside the house, the man who had held me so tenderly in his arms, whose one mission since I'd met him had seemed to be to keep me safe. Could he actually be a danger to me? Everything inside of me shouted "No!"

Simon had been with me when the shot destroyed the door and windows at my house. He'd warned me as soon as he'd seen movement outside and then flung himself forward to protect me as best he could. He'd been in every bit as much jeopardy as I had.

Or had he? I forced myself to think rationally. The shot wasn't fired until I crossed the room toward the backdoor. By that time Simon was well behind me. *I* was the target. Still, whoever shot at us was taking a big risk if they didn't want Simon dead along with me, especially by using a shotgun.

But Simon had wanted to leave me inside the house, determined to go after the shooter alone. He was the one who'd found Al's body outside in my yard. Was that happenstance? Or did he know where it was because he'd put it there? Was all of this some sort of elaborate charade to gain my trust?

I felt anger rise inside of me, replacing my fear. It made me want to go back inside and confront Simon Talbot or whoever the hell he was. But that wouldn't be wise, at least not until I knew more.

If Wes wasn't lying, his information could still be wrong. Even if he did have a note from Al, he could have misinterpreted it. I wasn't about to throw away what trust Simon and I had developed without evidence that Wes's accusations were true.

I forced myself to calm, feeling the coolness of the evening for the first time against the heat of my cheeks, and decided to find out for myself. Just inside the door, I grabbed the bag with my drives, my jacket, and my helmet. Then I stepped into the living room. Simon was sitting in his office chair with the soles of his boots pressed up against the edge of his desk.

I wanted desperately to tell him about Wes's accusation, to give him a chance to explain or to say Wes was making the whole thing up. But I didn't dare.

"I'm going out," I announced, forcing a smile and willing my voice to sound normal.

I slipped on my jacket and zipped it up.

"Where to?" he asked, watching me over his shoulder.

"I'm taking some footage to my producer. He needs to have them tonight," I said, hoping he wouldn't notice the sweat I felt beading on my forehead. I couldn't let Simon know I had any doubts about him or his identity. If what Wes had said *was* true, I certainly didn't want to send off alarms in Simon's head. And if it wasn't, I didn't want to hurt him.

"I thought you were talking to Claire."

"I was. Conrad beeped in." The lie tasted sour in my mouth.

"Want some company?" he offered with a slow smile.

"No, I'll be fine."

"When will you be back? It's late."

His words held the suggestion of a subtle third degree and a possible side to Simon I hadn't seen before. I pushed down my resentment about being questioned. I'd had a jealous husband. A relationship like that could get ugly. I had to play this right if I didn't want Simon to know I had any suspicions about him.

"Soon," I promised. I walked over to him, pushed his feet to the floor, and sat down on his lap facing him, straddling his legs. I leaned in and kissed him, long and sweet, with enough passion that he'd be sure I was coming back.

I could feel his posture relax as his anxiety eased.

Then I drew back. I stared into his eyes, searching for deceit, but I couldn't find any. I wanted so much for Wes to be wrong.

He touched the side of my cheek. "You okay? You look sad."

"I'm fine," I insisted, forcing a smile.

I had to remind myself I'd only known Simon for two days. Regardless of any feelings I might have for him, I really knew nothing about him.

"You sure you have to go?" he asked, holding onto my hand as I stood.

I pulled out of his grasp. I couldn't allow him to sway me. I had someone I had to see before I went to see Wes, someone I trusted implicitly. Someone who, I hoped, might help me sort this all out.

"You won't even have time to miss me," I assured him. At the door I turned back to take one last look at him, dreading what I might find out and wondering if I'd ever set foot in this house again.

"Thanks for the doughnuts," I said. "Save me a couple of the blueberry ones for when I get back."

"If Wes has Al's notes, he had to have taken them off of his body," I insisted as I paced in front of Wilma in her tiny living room in a small neighborhood a couple of blocks over from her office. Al didn't know Wes, and I couldn't imagine him trusting him with information intended for me.

She was ready for bed: flannel pajamas with cats printed all over the fabric, a worn terry cloth robe over that, and big, fuzzy blue slippers.

"Stop. You're making me dizzy," she said, putting her hand over her eyes.

I turned and looked at the woman as she sat on her flower print sofa that was older than I was. Her hair was wound around spongy pink curlers, and she had some sort of net over all of it. I hadn't seen anything like that since before my grandmother had died.

Her years were betraying her, made more apparent by her lack of make-up, which meant she had no visible eyebrows or eyelashes. But mostly it was her grief over the loss of her husband that lent her face a drawn look that hadn't been there two weeks ago. The lines around her eyes and mouth had deepened. Why had I thought…

"Wilma, I'm sorry. I shouldn't have barged in on you like—"

"Oh, pish!" she waved her hand at me. "You're kicking off my vertigo. Knock off the swishing back and forth, and I'll be fine."

"If I weren't here you'd probably—"

"Be bored out of my mind or thinking too much. I don't

get a lot of company in the evenings except for the pizza delivery guy, so I get ready for bed early. Doesn't mean I go to sleep. Got me a date with Jon Stewart every night at eleven on Comedy Central. So don't you fret about keeping me up. One o'clock is about my usual bedtime.

"Don't rule out the obvious," she suggested. "Al may have had a good reason to give the notes to Wes *before* he died."

"But why would he? And what if he didn't?"

"Do you think Wes killed Al?"

Her words were calm, as though she were talking about any murder victim, not her own husband.

I shook my head. "I don't know."

"C'mon, sweetie. Give my Al some credit. Whoever did him in had to be pretty darned clever."

I smiled. Wilma was right. Wes would have been no match for Al. Wes might be jealous, difficult, and occasionally undependable, but I'd never felt in any danger around him.

But then I'd never been a threat to him—at least not before now.

"Maybe what Wes told me about Simon isn't true," I said. "Maybe there are no notes. Maybe he was just trying to get me away from Simon."

"You think this may all be a ruse then?" Wilma asked, staring me straight in the eyes.

"Could be. Wes despises Simon."

Wilma humphed. "Jealous, huh? He'd have a right to be, assuming you and Wes ever—"

"Not for a long, long time."

"Young and foolish, eh?"

"Very young and incredibly foolish."

"So you want me to check it out independently, find out whether or not Simon is really Michael's brother."

"If you can."

Wilma nodded. "I gotta warn you, this may not be as

easy as you'd think. I'll try to look up a birth registration for him and see what I get, make a search for the mother. Did he say what state he was born in?"

"My guess would be Maryland, but you might check Pennsylvania as well. He claims his parents are Thomas and Janice Whitehall, that Whitehall was his stepfather. His birth father would be Talbot, but I don't have a first name."

"I don't suppose the Whitehalls have any living family."

"Not that I could find. I researched all the families for the documentary, but not in depth. I was looking for people to interview, not verifying lineage."

"All righty then," Wilma said. "I'll see what I can do. Used to be marriage certificates in some states listed whether or not the bride or groom had been previously married, but a lot didn't. Of course, folks can lie—on the record as well as off."

"Whatever Al had, he'd found it in less than a day on a weekend," I pointed out.

Wilma smiled and shook her head. "I'm no Al, baby cakes, but I'll do what I can. He was the best, you know."

"I do know."

I hugged her goodbye at the door.

"Where you off to?" she asked. "You aren't going back to Simon's, are you?"

"Wes asked me to meet him in Bethesda."

"Do you think that's wise?"

"Probably not, but Wes was with me the night Al died. My information ends when he and Isaacs and I walked out of the bar that evening."

I pulled open the door, but Wilma blocked my way. I could see true worry in her face for the first time.

"Someone tried to kill you, Eva. Don't forget that."

"Believe me, I won't."

"You don't have to go. You can stay here with me

tonight and for as long as you need to," she offered. "I'll keep you safe. We can call the authorities in the morning."

The image of Wilma defending me in her PJs, robe, and pink curlers brought a smile to my lips. I thought she might just be able to do it, too, but safe wasn't what I needed right now. And I was able to take care of myself. I moved past her before she could say anything that would break my resolve.

What Wilma didn't know was there had been a second attempt on my life, the one after I'd left Wes's apartment. Wes could easily have spotted me at his complex and followed me onto the George Washington Parkway, but where would he have gotten the Hummer?

The memory of blinding headlights in my rearview mirror sent a chill through me. But I had my bike this time, and I was not about to be caught in that sort of situation again. I could take it places no truck could go.

If Wes's phone call was an attempt to isolate me, he'd done a clever job, making certain I wouldn't tell Simon where I was going. What he wouldn't have counted on was my telling Wilma that I was meeting him. Jesse had taught me that. "Never," he always told me, "go somewhere without someone knowing where you are."

I ordered a caramel coffee and took up watch at a table near the front window where the cool evening air blew in every time the door opened, and I could see everyone who approached the coffee shop. I checked my watch. Wes was late. Of course he was. Had he ever been on time for anything in his life?

I should have been thinking about Wes and why it had taken him so long to call me back and what he'd been doing in the meantime. But my thoughts kept straying to Simon.

Of the August Eight, Michael Whitehall would have been my choice if I'd been choosing to impersonate a family member. Both of Michael's parents were dead. He had no siblings—assuming what Wes was saying was true—no one to stand up and say this man is an imposter. If someone wanted a way to work themselves into my confidence, I couldn't think of a better way to do it than assuming the identity of a nonexistent relative of Michael Whitehall.

But *why* would he do it? And could he have faked the emotional connection he seemed to have to Michael and his family? Or the one the two of us seemed to share? But if Simon wasn't Michael's brother, what stake could he have in finding the killer of the August Eight?

Even if he wasn't who he claimed he was, I was absolutely sure that Simon didn't mean me physical harm, at least not yet, which meant I must be valuable to him in some way.

He could easily have killed me in my sleep. Or that first night at my home when I walked into my kitchen, totally oblivious to his waiting for me in the dark. But why would he want me dead—unless he was the original killer and believed I would expose him through the making of my documentary. He certainly didn't seem to have any obvious connection to the current attempts on my life or Claire's. He'd been with me when Claire was shot at.

Why, then, if he were involved, would he introduce himself back into a situation he'd managed so successfully to escape, especially when I'd been so hell bent on getting Isaacs convicted?

I took the last sip of my coffee. I wouldn't find answers about Simon here.

I looked at my watch again. Wes had stood me up. Why had I thought he would show?

At least he was alive.

Or he had been a couple of hours ago.

And I knew the answer to one question that had haunted me since finding myself at the 7-Eleven: I hadn't somehow caused his death. For that I was grateful. It didn't mean, however, that I didn't want to kill him now.

I stood and threw my paper cup into the trash bin. I turned to find Wes right in my face. He grabbed my elbow and steered me toward the back of the shop.

I wrenched my arm free, anger boiling up inside of me.

"The only acceptable excuse for your not calling me back Monday morning would be your broken body lying in Suburban Hospital's ICU in a full body cast."

Wes slung his dark hair out of his eyes, a frown on his handsome face and several days' stubble on his chin. He looked like he hadn't showered or changed his clothes in days.

"Aw crap, Evie. Lighten up and sit down."

I sat and pulled him down with me, my fist wrapped around the collar of his jacket. I leaned close to his ear. "Do something to me like that one more time and the ICU is exactly where you'll find yourself. Now where the hell have you been?"

He pulled out of my grip. "I got me a room. Hell, Evie, someone's trying to kill us."

"Right. So what's this? Every man for himself?"

"Hell, no. I answered, didn't I?"

"Thanks. I've only left you a dozen messages. How did you get hold of Isaacs to arrange for him to meet us at the bar in Dupont?"

"His son left a note with a contact number under the windshield wiper of the van. I found it when I was loading up our equipment after our shoot Friday afternoon."

"Christopher Isaacs was there? At the filming?"

"Apparently."

"Why didn't you give it to me?" I demanded.

Wes clenched his jaw. "I thought if I set something up—"

"I'd be grateful? Are you kidding me? You scheduled a meeting with Isaacs and lured me to it without warning me?"

Wes would like to have earned my respect, but he had no idea how to do it.

"When I called him, Isaacs said all he wanted was a fair hearing. He preferred to talk to you face-to-face, and I told him I would arrange it. It seemed like the thing to do at the time."

"Well, it wasn't," I snapped.

"I was pretty sure I could get him to agree to talk to you on film. That was the only reason I called him without telling you. Think about it. You would have eaten him alive. And probably scared him off for good."

I rolled my eyes.

"What did he say at the bar?" I asked.

"Same old, same old. Nothing we hadn't heard before. He still denied any involvement in the murders. But he did agree to the interview."

"Really."

That surprised me. I wouldn't have thought I could have been civil enough to him to get him to agree. But I would have been talking to him after Simon had given me the psychiatric reports from the prison. According to Simon, by then I had begun to doubt Isaacs' guilt. Still, anything I got on film could be used against him in a court of law and he knew it. It was risky, not only for a guilty man but for an innocent one as well.

"How'd you get Al's notes?" I asked.

"His note. It was only one. He passed it to me in the bar Sunday night."

"To you?" I narrowed my eyes at him.

"He didn't want Isaacs to know he'd made contact with us. He slipped me a piece of paper as we passed by him on our way out."

"Isaacs knew who Al was. Christopher had made him at Isaacs' sister's house."

"So he knew he was being tailed? Well, Al didn't know

that. You were on the other side of Isaacs as we walked out. That's why Al gave it to me."

Al knew Wes from our work on the film, but he also knew what I thought of Wes, which meant whatever he had was important enough to risk having it go through him. He wanted me to get the information right away.

"Obviously, he meant me to give it to you," Wes went on, "but I didn't get the chance."

"Why not?"

"Because less than five minutes after you, me, and Isaacs walked out the door, it started raining bullets."

The thud of a silenced shot spit through my head. Followed by the flash of another. The memory was so vivid I felt a surge of panic rush through my body.

"Evie, what's wrong? You look sick."

I tried to shake it off. As quickly as it'd come, the sensation was gone. Nothing visual except the flash, but the sound was as real as if I'd just heard it. The experience left me dazed and my heart racing, as it had that night at the 7-Eleven.

I cleared my throat, hoping Wes hadn't sensed the anxiety that left me off balance.

"I'm fine. Where were we when we were shot at?" I asked.

"At the end of the alley on the east side of the bar."

"Where were we headed?"

"To my car. Neither you nor Isaacs had wheels, and you wanted to get him on film that night—before he had a chance to change his mind. We were going back to your place where we could set up your camera equipment. You really can't remember any of this?"

I shook my head. "Who shot at us?"

"I don't know. Hell, don't you think I would have told you first off if I'd had any idea."

"Was Isaacs hit?"

Blood. There'd been blood on my hands. Could Isaacs have died that night in the alley? If so, why hadn't his body been found and why couldn't I remember?

"I don't know."

"What do you mean, you don't know?" I demanded, cursing under my breath as I rapidly reached my frustration limit.

Suddenly I realized the answer before he spoke, and my anger surged again. I was on my feet, spitting words. "You took off, didn't you?"

"Sit down, Evie. We're in a public place."

He eyed the people around us, a couple of whom were frowning at us. As if Wes gave a damn about courtesy. But he was banking that I did.

I sat, not because I cared, but because there were too many witnesses. Who knows what I might have done to him if we'd been alone.

"We *all* scattered," he said.

"*Did* we?"

He shook his head.

He'd run and never looked back—*if* he was telling the truth. And he wouldn't have seen Al die if that's when it had happened.

I tried to soften my reaction. He'd panicked. Who was I to judge him? Maybe I had, too.

"How'd I get the bump on my head?" I asked.

"Blast it, Evie, I don't know. Shots were popping. We were all going a little crazy. After I got the message you left on my phone, I knew you were all right."

"All right? Someone took out a door and the windows in my kitchen with a shotgun. You bastard. Why didn't you call me back?"

"I was afraid you might be with Talbot."

"So? You think he was behind the ambush?"

"You got someone better? Isaacs was with us."

Another flash. This one of Isaacs' face. His features were contorted. Was it pain or was it rage? The memory was almost there...and then it slipped away as though it had never been there at all. My head hurt and I cursed again. Why couldn't I remember?

"Look, all I wanted to do was warn you. Don't trust that son-of-a-bitch Talbot."

"Because Al said so or because you don't like him. How do I know there ever was a note from Al?"

His hand burrowed into the pocket of his jeans and came up with a crumpled piece of paper. He threw it on the table.

"Here. This is it. Judge for yourself. Now I'm out of here."

"Tell me where you're staying," I called after him.

"No way, not if you're shacking up with that creep."

And with that he was gone. I didn't bother going after him. He'd be around, and I now knew he was at least checking his messages.

I unwadded the paper and flattened it against the table top. Scrawled in Al's distinct style of printing were these words:

Janice Dietrich Whitehall. Only marriage to Thomas F. Whitehall. Only one recorded offspring: Michael T. Whitehall.

My breath caught in my throat. Wes hadn't lied. Al had found the registration for Michael's birth, and listed on it had been Janice's maiden name. With that he would have traced all the recorded births of any children she might have had.

I shivered. If Simon wasn't Michael Whitehall's brother, who was he?

Chapter 15

"Simon—" I started.

"Eva. Where the hell are you? I've been half out of my mind with worry."

I covered the mouthpiece of my cell phone with my free hand while I tried to force myself to calm down. Just hearing his voice made my heart race. He sounded so sincere, so genuinely concerned. Was it real or just an act?

I wanted to demand an explanation. I wanted to scream *who are you* into the phone. Instead, I bit down hard on my lower lip and forced two breaths into my lungs.

"I'm sorry I didn't call sooner," I said as normally as I could manage. "I took the footage by Conrad's, but it turns out I'm going to have to edit some of these sequences together myself. It'll probably take most of the night."

I swallowed the distaste of my lie. A part of me still hoped that Al had somehow missed Simon's birth certificate. Maybe Simon had been born in a foreign country. Maybe I was making up ridiculous excuses when the facts were staring me in the face. I wasn't willing to risk everything on the remote possibility that the most competent P.I. I'd ever met had slipped up. I knew better.

Even while my instincts were still screaming for me to trust Simon.

"Do you really have to do that editing now?" he asked.

"There's a lot of money riding on this documentary, Simon."

"Of course. But why didn't you call?"

"I lost all track of time."

Another lie. It stung my throat.

"When are you coming home?"

Home. As though we shared his house together. As though it were still the haven it had been for me just hours ago.

"I don't know. It'll be easier if I just crash here for the night."

"At Conrad's?"

"No." I couldn't give him a real place. He might come looking for me. "At a friend's house near here. I've got to go. I'll call you later. I promise."

And with that I hung up, not trusting myself to tell Simon one more lie and go undetected. Or to keep my resolve to stay away from him. I shut off my cell phone and pulled on my helmet, my heart aching. I needed to get out of D.C.

I got Jackie out of bed by pounding on the carved oak of her front door. She opened it, barefoot, pulling the belt of a pink silk robe about her and shushing me. She didn't want me to wake her husband, but it was too late.

"Who the hell is out there? It's after one in the morning," I heard him roar from the hallway, as she pulled me inside.

"Go back to bed, Rick. It's all right. It's only Eva."

"Doesn't she know what time it is? Tell her to go home and come back in the daytime—when I'm at work."

She rolled her eyes, shutting and locking the door behind me, then resetting the alarm.

"What's wrong?" she asked. Her hair was a mess and her eyes aflame with fear. "Are you all right? Has there been another shooting? Has Claire gotten worse? I took a fruit basket to her this afternoon. She seemed all right then."

"No, nothing's wrong. Claire's fine. I'm fine."

But she could see that I was shaking.

"Find me some caffeine and I'll fill you in," I promised.

It took me less than twenty minutes to tell her what had

happened with Simon and Wes over the last couple of days, while we drank some truly nasty instant coffee at her kitchen table. As she pointed out, I was lucky to get anything that required more than popping a lid. Jackie didn't cook or make coffee, even though she had a three-hundred dollar espresso machine sitting on her kitchen counter.

"You actually went off with some strange guy to his house without knowing anything about him?"

She let out a string of expletives in Spanish, only a few of which I could translate, but their meaning was perfectly clear.

"He's a cop," I insisted as though that somehow was enough reason for me to do what I'd done. Simon's badge had helped reassure me, but it hadn't been why I'd gone with him. I'd felt a connection to him. I'd thought the man was sincere. It was unsettling to think I might have been so wrong.

Pride made me refuse to give Jackie any reason to believe that I now doubted Simon might not really be Simon Talbot, the cop from Pittsburgh, if not Michael Whitehall's brother. She was already furious at me for not coming to her instead of going home with him. Besides, I didn't believe a man would sleep with a woman one moment and then blow her away the next.

Then I reminded myself, some of them do.

"He's more than a cop to you," Jackie said. "Just look at you. You're really upset. Are you hung up on this guy?"

"Of course not. I've only known him a couple of days." I hid my hands beneath the table so she couldn't see them tremble.

She gave me that who's-fooling-who look of hers. "If you're sleeping with this jerk—"

I felt the blood surge to my face.

"Jackie, I came here because I need your help, not your criticism." I stood up, my coffee only half finished. "If you're not—"

"I am. Now sit down. You're staying with me until we get this all sorted out."

Jackie was hot tempered, but she was very self aware and true to her word. I wouldn't hear any more recriminations, at least not about having stayed with Simon. The fact that I was safe now was enough for her.

But I couldn't sit down. My body was filled with so much nervous energy I couldn't be still. Instead, I stood shifting my weight back and forth against her expensive Italian tile as I voiced my worst fears.

"Simon may be in league with Isaacs," I said.

"You're kidding me. Are you sure?"

"No, but I don't think meeting Simon at that bar Saturday night could have been a coincidence, not with the number of bars in D.C. Only the three of us—Wes, Isaacs, and me—knew we were meeting. I know Wes didn't tell him. It must have been Isaacs."

"Do you really believe that?"

"I don't know," I answered honestly.

I felt a chill sweep through me as something Wes had said came back to me. "Simon could have been the one who ambushed Wes, Isaacs, and me in the alley Sunday night."

Jackie frowned.

"Think about it," I insisted. "Simon dropped me off near Dupont Circle, so I know he was downtown. What if Isaacs had told him we were meeting there again? What if he waited for us outside? What if his plan was to kill me that night?"

My mind was racing. "What if Simon killed Al and transported his body back to my house in *my* Jeep? He would have had plenty of time to dump Al's body in my backyard before you brought me home."

I never would have thought to ask the police to look in my Jeep for trace evidence. And now that it had been totaled, no one would have.

I felt like a fool. I'd made plenty of mistakes with men, but none of them had been killers. Could I really have been that far off base with Simon? He didn't have the eyes of a killer. I'd stared into too many of them in my interviews for my documentaries. He wasn't cold like that. He wasn't cold at all.

"Let's say you're right," Jackie suggested. "But if Simon wants you dead, why aren't you? He must have had any number of opportunities to kill you."

"I don't know unless he didn't want me showing up dead at his house. How easy would it be to know exactly where I'd be at any given time if I was staying with him, to manipulate me into being where he wanted me? If one attempt failed, he could have simply set up another."

I didn't dare utter the other thought that had plagued me since leaving Wes. Could Simon have been behind the wheel of that Hummer?

I'd seen his driving ability. He knew how to handle a car. I swallowed hard. The sheer power behind that attack, the relentless desire to smash me into oblivion...

I'd told myself Simon wasn't a psychopath, but any man who would sleep with a woman one moment and hunt her down the next was exactly that. So why couldn't I simply let myself believe it?

My eyes stung. Could the man who had kissed away my tears and then cradled me gently in his arms be the one who had sent my Jeep spinning out of control? I cringed at the thought. Were my instincts really that poor?

"You're exhausted," Jackie said, grabbing my hand. "Look at you. You can't even think straight. Let me get you settled in the guest room. You can borrow one of my nightgowns."

I hoped she was right. I hoped that my mind was twisting facts, and Simon wasn't the monster I feared he might be. I had to have some rest before I could think clearly.

"We'll get this sorted out in the morning," she promised. "Have you called Jesse?"

Jesse. He was the last person I wanted involved at the moment. I'd never hear the end of it if he knew that I'd been staying with Simon.

"I didn't want to wake him," I said.

"So you woke me instead."

"Sorry about that," I said sheepishly. "He'd just send an officer over here and what would I tell him? My dead P.I. said Simon wasn't really Michael's brother? Lying's not a punishable offense."

"It is in my house. And I refuse to accept any apology from you. The only thing you have to be sorry about is not coming here in the first place. Now get yourself to bed."

"Rick's not going to be happy if he wakes up and finds me here."

"Don't worry about him. I'll have him up and off to work before you even open your eyes. Besides, right now you and I are a package deal. If Rick wants me in this house, he damn well better want you."

I thought I'd never get to sleep. Simon had to be wondering where I was and why I'd disappeared. I pulled the pillow over my head and tried to think about anything except the man who was haunting my every thought.

I must have somehow finally managed to drift off because when Jackie brought in the scrambled eggs, toast, orange juice, and coffee her cook had made, I had trouble waking up.

I pushed myself up against the headboard of the sleigh bed, rubbing my eyes. She pulled back the down-filled comforter and set the tray across my lap. Then she sat herself down on the other side of the bed, munching on some grapes.

"I called Jesse. He's on his way over."

I stopped in mid chew. "I wish you hadn't done that."

"Why? Jesse's the one person who can help us. I told him no active duty police officers. Anything we have to say to him is to be kept in confidence until you decide otherwise."

Intellectually I knew she was right, that we had to involve Jesse, but I didn't want him directing my every move. He hadn't been able to figure out what had happened fifteen years ago. Why should I trust him to do it now?

And as good as Jesse had been to me, a part of me resented him. He'd let me down. He'd let us all down. I was just now beginning to realize how much that colored my feelings for him.

"I'm going to have the police put a guard on the house," Jesse insisted after I'd explained what happened with Simon. "And I don't want you going anywhere."

He sipped coffee Jackie's cook had offered him as we sat in her elegant living room.

I shook my head. "Nobody, except you, knows I'm here."

"And I don't think a police presence in this neighborhood is a good idea," Jackie added.

"It's the first place I looked when she disappeared after the shooting at her house," Jesse said.

"And I told you what I'd tell anybody coming to my door: she's not here, and I don't know where she is," Jackie said, with one eyebrow raised.

Jesse bristled. "Lying to me—"

"Okay, okay," I intervened. "Jackie didn't lie to you, Jesse. I wasn't here and you only knew to come here because you know all about me."

"And you think Isaacs doesn't know every person you're likely to associate with? How do you think he was occupying his time in prison? He was planning what he was going to do when he got out. That means studying you and everyone who had a hand in putting him in that institution in the first place. Sounds like this Simon Talbot is definitely in league with him."

Jesse was full blast into police mode. He'd even dressed the part, wearing the same sport jacket he'd had on at the hospital. He may have retired two years ago, but someone talking to him would never know it. Being a cop was in his blood.

"You've got to let us do our job," he insisted.

I wanted to say it's not your job anymore, but I didn't. He believed the August Eight was still his case. And as far as he was concerned, he'd solved it. He was absolutely convinced of Isaacs' guilt. The only reason I'd ever doubted it, he assured me, was because Simon had tried to make me think otherwise.

"How's your memory?" he asked.

"I've had a few flashes but so far only bits and pieces that don't make any sense. I remember the shots in the alley."

"But not who shot at you."

I shook my head.

Jesse patted my hand. "You lie low with Jackie and let me take it from here. Call me the minute you remember anything more. Understand? *The minute*. I've got this Simon Talbot's address." He patted his shirt pocket. "I'll get someone to pick him up right away."

"Jesse..." I started.

My indecision must have shone in my face.

"What is it?"

I got up and went over to the bag that had my drives in it and drew out a beer bottle I'd swiped out of Simon's trash on the way out the door.

"See if you can get someone to run these fingerprints. I'm not sure Simon Talbot is his real name."

A smile spread across Jesse's face. "You did good."

Then he stood and turned to Jackie. "Don't let her out of this house."

"I'll do what I can, but you know her," Jackie said.

"I mean it, Jackie. If you care about this girl—"

"I'm on it."

"I'll let you know the moment I get the results back on these prints."

I couldn't wait for Jesse to be gone. I was no girl, and I didn't need anyone doing my thinking for me. I waited only long enough for him to pull out of the driveway before I put on my jacket and grabbed my helmet.

"Where do you think you're going?"

"I can't tell you. If Jesse finds out, he might employ truth serum to get it out of you. But I promise I won't be long. Can I hook up a laptop to one of your nine televisions?"

"Sure. Whatever you need. And I only own eight TVs."

"Great. All I need is one. Warm it up for me while I'm gone."

"Need some company?" Jackie offered. "I took a self-defense class once. I know how to break an instep with my heel, and I understand a stiletto can put out an eye with the proper kick."

The image of Jackie attacking some thug with her Manolo Blahniks brought a smile to my lips. Who knew they were lethal weapons?

Besides, I already had someone helping me, someone who was a little lower maintenance.

"I'll see you when I get back," I told her, kissing her cheek. "And if you dare call Jesse, I'll throttle you."

Wilma looked much better than she had last night. The pink curlers had given her short, white hair waves, and she'd even put on some lipstick. I sat on the edge of the oak desk in the only spot that wasn't covered with papers. I handed her the note from Al that Wes had given me.

She read it and then looked up at me. "That's how I have it figured, too, from what I could find out. That's why I decided to come at Talbot from the other direction. I spent the morning seeing what I could find out about Simon Talbot, Pittsburgh P.D."

"I didn't expect you to have anything yet." I looked away, dreading what she might say.

"They think a lot of him up in Pittsburgh, but he hasn't been in touch with anybody since he took leave."

So we knew nothing more than I had days ago.

"I'm having a little trouble finding any record of his birth," Wilma added.

That brought me to full attention.

"I found one Simon Talbot about the right age but he wasn't born anywhere near this area. And I haven't found anything to connect him to the Whitehalls. His birth parents are listed as Talbots. If it's him, the mother's name is wrong. I'll keep looking."

I swallowed hard. Some part of me continued to hope Simon was who he'd said he was, even if he wasn't Michael's brother.

I stood up.

"If's there's any way you can do it, get Pittsburgh to fax you a photo of Talbot."

"I'll see what I can do," Wilma promised, "but it may take a while."

"Thanks. I need to get back to Jackie's. I've got some interviews to review."

Wilma's round cheeks pulled into a smile that lifted the end of her nose. "If I decide to keep the agency open after this is all over with, I'm going to have an opening for a partner."

I reached across the desk and squeezed her hand. "As tempting as that offer may be, I've got a documentary to finish."

"You'll need an ending. Can't do that before you know who's guilty," she said.

"Can't do that if I'm dead," I added under my breath.

Chapter 16

On the way back to Jackie's I pulled my bike over to the side of the road and called Simon. He'd left a short, almost brusque message asking me to call him back. The last thing I wanted was for him to become suspicious of me.

"Miss me?" I asked when he answered his cell.

"Where are you?"

I could hear the desperation in Simon's voice. I wanted so much to go to him, but I didn't dare.

"In transit. I've got some leads I'm running down," I said.

"Need some help?"

"Not yet. I'll let you know when."

For a moment neither of us said a word. I held my breath, terrified that he would finally tip his hand, and I would hear hatred in his voice.

"Yes," he said softly.

"Yes, what?"

"Yes, I miss you."

Then he hung up, leaving me with a hollow pit in my stomach, feeling as though I had betrayed him and not the other way around.

Jackie had the big screen TV on and waiting for me in her family room. She even threw in popcorn. She was pretty good at putting bags in the microwave, pushing buttons, and pouring the slightly burnt results into a bowl.

I supplied the entertainment. Interviews for my documentary. Surely, somewhere amidst the raw footage was something I'd missed.

First up: Drew Davis. Davis lived in an aging brick house in a middle-class neighborhood. He'd been about Michael's age when they'd graduated from the police academy together. What had struck me first when Ben and I had pulled into his driveway in Baltimore, where he now worked on the police force, were the tricycle and the scooter on the sidewalk leading up to the front door. This was the life that Michael might have had if he'd lived. I had Ben get several shots of the yard before we went in.

Davis had answered the door in full uniform, as crisply fresh and pleated as if he were leaving for his shift, not coming off of it. I'd wanted his family on film, but he wouldn't allow his boys, six and eight, to be photographed. His wife had taken them to her mother's home while we'd worked. I understood. As much as I wanted to, I wouldn't be using the footage of the toys or anything else that might identify the house.

I began with, "Michael wasn't on the force very long before he was killed."

Ben had caught all of Davis's emotion as he zoomed in for a close-up while Davis sat on the leather sofa in his den. Even now, after so many years had passed, the viewer could see the constriction in the throat of this man who dealt with crime every day. He swallowed it back before he spoke.

"We were both about as green as it gets." The half smile on his lips was perfect. "I still can't believe he died that way after what had happened only a couple of weeks before."

Michael Whitehall was a hero, which made it even more distasteful that someone would pretend to be his brother. And more surprising that his family had refused an official burial to honor his death, especially since his father was an officer himself.

"Michael was using a black and white to transport a witness from a designated safe house to the court house to testify that afternoon," I said. I knew the story well.

"Yes, ma'am."

"Tell me what happened."

"Michael and his partner were jumped on a busy, two-lane section of Route 28 about two miles from the courthouse. A large, white, windowless van suddenly pulled halfway out of a driveway and directly in front of them into the heavy traffic and stopped, blocking them in. The oncoming lane was filled with traffic, leaving the cruiser nowhere to go. Two gunmen armed with machine guns and wearing ski masks exited the vehicle and started firing."

The audacity of the attack was incredible, especially in a county as well patrolled as Montgomery.

"Who was driving?" I asked.

"Officer Rhodes. The witness they were transporting stated that Officer Whitehall shouted for him to get down on the floorboard. Rhodes was already dead, shot in the first round of bullets. Whitehall got out of the car and returned fire."

"On a busy street?"

"It was either that or let them kill the witness and who knows how many civilians. Michael took out one of the gunmen. The other one got away on foot. He was never apprehended."

"So there was a body to identify."

I'd wanted every detail he could give on tape.

"Yes, ma'am. Joseph Smits. He was a petty thief with a drug and alcohol problem. We were never able to link him directly to Paul O'Brien, who was on trial for embezzlement and the man that the witness was to testify against."

"Why was this such an important case?" I asked.

"We suspected O'Brien was behind the murder of a county official a few months prior, but we had no case against him. It was imperative, therefore, that we get a conviction on the embezzlement charge. That would allow us to keep O'Brien from fleeing the country while we waited for a break in the murder case."

"And who was the witness?"

"A co-worker of O'Brien's who realized he might be implicated in the embezzlement if he didn't cooperate."

As Jackie and I watched, I wondered if there'd ever been an investigation into the possibility that Luther Isaacs had known Joseph Smits. Someone had hired Smits and another person to ambush the police car. Was it insane to consider that Isaacs, who fit the same profile as Smits, might have been the second gunman who ambushed the patrol car transporting the witness?

I pressed the pause button and stared at the frozen screen. I wished there was someone to give me a physical description of the second gunman, but the only witnesses—Officers Rhodes and Whitehall—were dead.

"Are you actually getting something out of watching this?" Jackie asked.

"Aren't you?"

She threw a kernel of popcorn at my head and wasn't at all pleased that I acted as though it hadn't happened. My thoughts were elsewhere.

Paul O'Brien had fleeced his company of most of its profits for the preceding five years. If he could have beaten the charges against him, he would have left the U.S. with several million dollars of other people's money he'd hidden in offshore accounts. He could have met the price of almost anyone who had been willing to sell him their services to ambush Michael's cruiser.

But he hadn't beaten the charges. Thanks to Michael Whitehall, the witness had testified.

I pressed rewind.

"Oh, come on. Drew Davis is good looking, but really," Jackie said.

"You don't have to sit with me," I said. "But if you stay, you have to be quiet."

"Jesse ordered me to keep an eye on you."

We watched the interview again, this time letting it go all the way to the end. I wished I had Davis in front of me now, so I could ask him all the questions I should have asked him about whether or not there could be any possible connection between the ambush and the shooting death of Michael Whitehall.

He couldn't have answered my questions. Davis wouldn't know. He hadn't been part of the investigative team.

Instead Davis talked about Michael. How bright he was, how full of promise, how much he was missed. What he might have done with his life.

By the time I'd seen the interview a third time, Jackie had had enough. She spoke up.

"Okay, he kind of makes me wish I'd known Michael, but I can't figure out what you're getting out of watching this over and over. What am I missing?"

Questions were forming in my mind, but I didn't want to share them with anyone just yet, not even Jackie.

"This is the sort of thing you have to do when you make documentaries," I warned her. "Think we could get some sodas to go with our popcorn?"

She rolled her eyes and stood up. "I'm indulging you only because I want you to stay here. Cola or ginger ale?"

"Cola."

I queued up Jesse's interview as she left the room. I fast forwarded to the part where I'd asked him about Michael.

If Simon wasn't who he said he was, what was his link to Michael? I was growing more and more certain there was a reason he'd presented himself as Michael's brother. He wanted to gain my trust and it had worked, but was there more? I had no doubt Simon had a vested interest in this case. What I needed to do was find out what it was. And which side he was on.

"Michael Whitehall was a fine young officer with an

outstanding career in front of him. To have his life cut short in a senseless string of random murders was both tragic and ironic. He accepted responsibility normally reserved for much more seasoned officers, using his ability and clear thinking. That's why I assigned him to that detail. It was a pity he had to die."

I watched Jesse's face as he spoke. Michael's death appeared to have touched him deeply. He seemed to react more like a family member than a police officer with none of the detachment I'd expected from officials involved in this case. But then Jesse had become attached to most of us affected by the deaths. In those first few months after the murders, he'd spent many of his off duty hours with us.

He also spoke about Isaacs and his fears of what might happen when he was released. He mentioned warning the families to be on alert. He and I certainly had had several hours of discussion about it. He also warned me, off camera, to drop the whole idea of doing my documentary. Barring that, he offered to give me personal protection while I was working on it.

I was ready to rewind Jesse's tape and play it through again, despite Jackie's obvious boredom, when her telephone rang.

She handed me the phone. It was Jesse asking to speak to me.

I tossed my popcorn bowl onto the end table and sat up, quickly brushing the salt off of my fingers.

"Did you get a hit on the fingerprints?" I asked.

"You're not going to like this," Jesse said.

"Just tell me."

"Is Jackie still there with you?"

"Yeah. Do you want me to put you on speaker phone?"

"No. I want you to go into another room. Everything I'm about to say is to stay between you and me. Understand?"

I threw a look in Jackie's direction. She held up her

hands. "I guess I know when I'm not wanted."

I waited for her to cross into the kitchen. "All clear."

I took a deep breath and steeled myself for what I was about to hear.

"The fingerprints on the beer bottle you gave me don't match Simon Talbot's."

I swallowed hard. I didn't want to give Jesse any hint as to how emotionally involved I'd become with Simon. "What's his name?"

I could hear the intake of air over the phone. "The only hit we got was for the second group of prints left in the van at the ambush of Whitehall's cruiser in the O'Brien case. Those prints were never identified. We don't even have a name."

My heart sped faster in my chest, as blood pounded in my ears. "You're absolutely certain?"

"Fingerprints don't lie, Eva. I wish I had better news for you."

I choked back tears, forcing my voice to sound halfway normal. "Have you picked him up?" I didn't even have a name for Simon.

"He's not at his house. I asked the Alexandria P.D. to put a unit out there to watch the place, in case he comes back."

"He has a police badge. Jesse."

"Simon Talbot *is* a cop in Pittsburgh, but he's been missing for over a month. It's possible your guy may have killed Talbot and assumed his identity."

Killed him. The words rang in my ears. Could Simon actually be a cold-blooded killer? Of a police officer?

"At the very least this guy bought the badge off of some hood," Jesse continued. "Do you remember his badge number?"

At the moment, I could barely remember my own name.

"No. But if he was part of the Whitehall ambush, and he" — I almost choked on the word — "killed Talbot, what's he doing here?"

"I don't know unless he's got some link to Isaacs," Jesse offered.

"I thought Isaacs always worked alone."

"We did, too, but there was one theory floating around the department that the August Eight was a two-man job. And if this mystery 'Talbot' is involved with Isaacs, that could mean Whitehall's death wasn't random."

It was one of Simon's theories as well. But was it only a theory for him or did he know it to be true because he'd been in on the killings? Why would he tell me that? He'd said he'd seen all of my documentaries. Was he playing me? Was he so damned arrogant he was sure he could feed me little pieces of the truth and get away with it? I swallowed back bile. I didn't have the luxury of being sick.

I felt myself grow cold. Christopher Isaacs' appearance at Simon's house…I'd come home earlier than Simon had expected. Had I walked in on one of their strategy sessions? The noise from my bike would have warned them I was there, giving them just enough time to concoct a story I'd believe.

"And the current attacks?" I managed.

"I think you know the answer."

"But why would they do it?" I begged.

"They know you want Isaacs convicted. You weren't very discreet in your comments to the press or at his parole hearings. They want to stop you before you have enough evidence to do just that, and before you uncover the involvement of Isaacs' accomplice."

Jesse had placed the blame for the attack on Claire squarely on my shoulders. I felt myself sag under its weight.

"I want you in a safe house," Jesse insisted. "I'll arrange something. I can come get you."

"How will you get him if I go into hiding?"

"I don't know, but we'll have to find a way to draw him out. If we don't, more people will be hurt."

It was all on me—not only Claire's injuries, but the responsibility for any future attacks. How could I live with myself if I didn't do something?

"I think Simon still trusts me. I've been in touch with him by phone." I cleared my throat. "I should be able to set up something. It may be the only way to bring him in."

"I can't let you do that, Eva."

"How many years have you known me, Jesse?" I asked.

"Point taken. Okay, but we'll have to keep you safe, understand?"

"That's the plan."

"Do you know if he's currently in contact with Isaacs?"

"He has to be. And if he's not directly, he's in touch with Isaacs' son Christopher."

"We need them both—Isaacs and Simon."

"I understand. I'll let you know when and where I plan to meet them."

"You're not calling the shots on this one," Jesse insisted.

But I refused to be bullied. I could feel some of my strength replacing the shock that had overwhelmed me. "This meeting will be on my terms, or I'm hanging up this phone."

I was sure he was furious with me. Several seconds passed before he responded.

"All right. But it needs to be tonight and away from any populated areas. Keep it in the county so when we call in the police, they'll have jurisdiction to handle it. I don't want any civilians getting hurt. Call me as soon as you've made contact with him."

"You got it."

"Eva, be careful. Don't tell anyone, not even Jackie. We don't have any real proof at this point."

"You've got his fingerprints. Isn't that enough for a warrant?"

"Yes, but we need more."

"I'll get it for you. You'll have my back?"

"I will."

I hung up Jackie's phone, pulled out my cell, checked the recent calls menu, and found Simon's number. It was under the name of Simon Talbot. I wondered if I was calling a dead man's phone. I held my breath for several seconds before I called.

He answered on the first ring.

"Simon, it's Eva. Where are you?"

"Don't worry. I'm fine."

"You're not at home then."

"No. Someone's been at my house. I think they're watching the place. I can't be answering a lot of questions right now from anybody. Whoever's been doing these shootings is getting desperate. But at least you're safe."

"Yes." I closed my eyes and swallowed hard. I could hear what sounded like genuine concern in the gentle timbre of his voice. I bit my lip. If he were lying to me, it seemed to come easily. But my lying to Simon was hard.

"I need to see you," I said.

"I'll come get you. Just tell me where you are."

"No!" I said louder than I'd intended, and then calmed. "You can't come here. But somewhere close. Do you know Great Falls Park on the Maryland side?"

"Sure. What of it?"

"Can we make it there later tonight?"

"Eva, what are you doing? How about now at the restaurant we ate at in Rockville?"

"Listen to me," I insisted. "This is the safest way. The park closes at dark. Meet me at nine near the Tavern. It's the only large structure in the park. It houses a museum and the restrooms, and it's close to the entrance. You really can't miss it.

"You need to find a way to get Isaacs there, too," I went on. "He's got the answers we need."

"But we don't even know how to reach him."

"Don't we? Can't you call Christopher?" I dug the slip of paper he'd left me at Simon's house and read off the phone number on it, removing any excuse he might make up about not knowing how to contact Isaacs.

"I'll see what I can do, but I don't know if he'll come."

"Tell him if he's innocent, this is the only way to clear his name."

"Okay, I'll try. But why all this secrecy? What are you planning, Eva?"

There was something new in his voice. A hardness. Had he begun to doubt me?

"Whatever I have to do to get to the bottom of what happened fifteen years ago."

Chapter 17

I stood shivering in the cold, despite the leather of my jacket and gloves. My gun weighed heavily inside the back waistband of my jeans as my back rested against a tree trunk. I wondered if Simon would show, even while I almost hoped he wouldn't. He had to be one hell of a con man to have fooled me so completely. A part of me hated him for it. Another part still refused to believe I had been fooled. Could anyone fake the feelings we'd shared? Could my instincts really have been so wrong?

I stared into the darkness, feeling my jaw tighten. Jesse was out there somewhere. He'd told me he'd be here with his men in place by eight o'clock. I'd seen nothing to indicate a police presence when I'd driven up and left my bike at the end of the lot, but that was the way it was supposed to be. Simon's car was also nowhere to be seen. I assumed I'd arrived first.

Isaacs should be along, too, if Simon had done what I'd asked him to do. I felt as though I was on some kind of roundup, and I was the bait in the center of it all. This wasn't my style.

But it was my battle.

When I'd called Jesse back confirming the meeting with Simon, he'd laid out a plan. I was to engage Simon and get him to follow me to a designated spot a little further up the trail that bordered the C & O Canal. A bridge led over toward a lookout onto the Potomac and the falls. We were to stop there.

Jesse would be there waiting in the dark. He and I would get the drop on Simon together, as the police moved in and cut off the only way back to the road.

The only thing missing was the Judas kiss.

I itched for a cigarette. I hadn't had one in over twelve years. But if I'd had one on me, I would have been smoking it. I needed something to calm my nerves. The thought of seeing Simon again, knowing his deceit, left my heart racing with anger. I had to control my feelings, or Simon would know something was wrong.

The tavern stood about forty feet away as I watched from the wooded area on the other side of the wide path near the canal. The moon was full, casting a yellow light across the open areas. But in the trees it was as black as midnight, even with so many of the fall leaves already on the ground.

The crunch of boots on gravel startled me, and I looked to my right. A lone man was approaching from the direction opposite the parking lot. That was wrong. Simon should have come from the other way. That's where I'd told him to leave his car.

The figure stopped, mostly in shadow, across the paved area, almost directly in front of the tavern. He was about the right height and girth for Simon, too husky to be Christopher, too tall and sure of his movements to be Isaacs. I could tell from his silhouette that he was wearing a short jacket, like Simon's leather one. He shifted back and forth on the balls of his feet. I could feel his tension from here. I shared it with him.

I took a deep breath, wishing I was anywhere else, and stepped into the moonlight. He saw me immediately.

"Simon," I called out as I approached, thankful my face was in shadow and trying to keep my voice light. I wanted to alert Jesse that I'd made contact. My every step seemed to echo on the pavement. He waited until I stopped, only ten feet separating us, before he spoke.

"Eva. What the hell is this all about? Why didn't you come back to the house last night? What's with all this secrecy?"

The anger in his voice sent chills through me. I didn't

know this side of Simon. I didn't want to know it.

He started toward me, reaching out, but I drew back, loathe to have him touch me, not when I had set him up. And not when I knew the hands that had wiped my tears may have also taken a man's life.

"Were you able to contact Isaacs?" I asked in a loud whisper.

"He'll be here."

"I don't want him to know we're in this together."

"And what is it we're in together? What are you up to?"

His sharp words bit into me. I was glad I couldn't see the distrust that had to be burning in his eyes.

"I told you Isaacs isn't your man," Simon lashed out. "He didn't commit those murders. He didn't shoot at you or Claire, and he didn't kill Al."

"How can you be so sure?" I asked.

Unless he knew who did.

"You've been talking to someone," he accused. "Who?"

A second set of footsteps silenced us both as we turned to look. It had to be Isaacs. The man's white hair was frizzed and reflected the light in a glow around his head, leaving his entire face in shadow. He limped as he haltingly made his way toward us.

"Ms. Keller," he called out. His voice was breathy and almost familiar, and surprisingly loud in the night air.

My body bristled at finally coming face-to-face with this man. But when he came closer, even in the dark, I could see how debilitated he looked. His shabby trousers hid the reason for his limp. His arm was in some sort of homemade sling, and his hand shook. When and how had he been hurt? Was this pathetic creature the devil of my nightmares?

Instinctively, I stepped forward to steady him. He seemed too frail to be a threat to anyone. His hand wrapped around my wrist as he caught his breath.

"What happened to you?" I asked.

I saw the surprise on his face, now partially illuminated in the moonlight. He had an old man's face, one that I knew. I'd seen it, not just in photos, but in my dreams.

A bullet spat in the silence, tearing through Isaacs' upper arm and spraying his blood all over my hand. Terror strangled my throat as Isaacs slid to the ground, his hand losing grasp of my wrist. For a second, I stood frozen as I stared transfixed at the stickiness on my palm. It was covered with Isaacs' blood.

Simon's first "Get down" sounded muffled, as though it were coming from far away. The second was in my ear as he pushed me to the ground and into the shadows. I crouched paralyzed as memory flooded through me.

We were walking, about halfway down the length of the alley beside the bar, Wes and me on either side of Isaacs. A shot flew past my left ear. Suddenly, Wes was gone, running, not looking back, as fast as he could down the alley. I cursed and turned, ducking a second shot. I saw our assailant as time stopped — a short, slim figure wearing a black ski mask and gloves shooting at us from the corner of the bar's Dumpster at the mouth of the alley. His rifle aimed once more. I knew I was in his sights. Isaacs moved near me as the shot sounded. He went down, and I sank with his weight. I saw his face, twisted in pain, staring up at me. The blood oozed from his shoulder. My hands were covered in it, as I knelt and pressed desperately against the wound to stop the bleeding. Words fell from my lips to ring in my own ears.

"David. Please, God, David, don't die."

I staggered to my feet in horror and ran. I ran from death, ran from the memory, ran from myself. I didn't stop running until I fell, pitching forward, my head hitting concrete. I dragged myself up and still I ran, until I found myself at the 7-Eleven.

Another bullet spat through the night air, and I was back in Great Falls Park.

Simon shook me hard. "Snap out of it."

Suddenly I knew all I needed to know. Simon had not been the shooter in the alley beside the bar. He hadn't killed Al. And neither had Isaacs. I wanted to tell him, but there was no time.

He dragged me forward until I found my footing. The shots were to our left, so we plunged right, running on the pavement. But we were too exposed by the moonlight. Another shot sounded. Simon pulled me into the brush as more shots followed us.

"He's using a high-powered rifle, and my bet is he has a night scope," Simon said.

I drew the gun from my waistband and turned to face our assailant. But everything was dark. I had no idea where he was.

Simon grabbed my arm and pushed me forward once more. Still dazed, I found my feet on wood. We were on one of the bridges on the wooden footpath that crossed the small inlets and led to the lookout over the falls.

And the shooter was closing in. Where was Jesse? Where were the police?

As I gasped for breath, I realized we had no options. We were being herded by the monster behind the rifle.

"Who's out there?" Simon demanded.

Could something have happened to Jesse? Who else would know we were here?

"Jesse Sedwick's supposed to be," I managed, my breath short.

"Jesse?" Simon sounded truly surprised.

"You met him at the hospital when we went to see Claire."

"I know exactly who he is. Why would he be here?"

"Isaacs. Jesse intended to have him arrested if he showed."

I couldn't let on that I knew about Simon's involvement

with Isaacs. At this point, all that mattered was that I knew Simon wasn't in league with the person who'd been trying to kill me. Regardless of any crimes he might have committed in the past, I believed in my heart Simon was no killer.

"Could someone have followed you?" I asked Simon.

"I don't think so."

"Maybe someone followed Isaacs," I suggested.

Or maybe me. Anyone who knew me could have guessed that I'd be at Jackie's. Had someone been watching her house? Could Jesse have had it all wrong? Where was he? Dead?

My mind was spinning, desperately trying to come up with any explanation other than the one that sent an icy chill down my spine. Was Jesse the shooter?

"Simon, I remember what happened in the alley. I remember Isaacs getting shot. I know he's not behind the shootings."

He shushed me. "Move or we'll both be dead."

I sucked in air and raised my gun. All that mattered right now was that I knew Simon was innocent. And so was Isaacs.

And that I refused to be another number in this murderer's tally.

Anger tensed all of my muscles, as we sprinted across a second bridge, the blackness on either side hiding the water below. It'd be harder for our pursuer now to stay hidden. He'd have to follow the wooden trail just as we had if he wanted to come after us. The roar of the rapids ahead was growing louder. We were nearing the river.

The trail ended in a fenced-in overlook, trapping us. The rushing river thundered below, its silvery surface glittering in reflected moonlight.

Directly below the deck, in the shadows, were large, jagged rocks. We were trapped like cattle in a corral.

"What do we do now?" I asked.

"We've only got two directions: forward or back."

As if on cue, another shot flew past.

"Back is not an option."

"Get rid of your gun," Simon ordered.

I shoved it into my jeans, as he holstered his. I was already scrambling to the top of the railing. He grabbed my arm and spun me toward him, taking hold of my elbows as I wrapped my hands around the crooks of his arms.

"Hang on," he warned. "I'll drop you as far as I can."

Then he bent over the railing as I kicked off. He lowered me at the corner support post. With a prayer, I reclaimed one arm and wrapped it around the thick wood, thankful I was wearing gloves. Everything below me was black. I had no idea how far down the ground might be. I did know that a miscalculation could send me heading straight down the rock face toward the churning waters.

Simon released my other elbow, and I reached for the support, hugging it tightly. I tried to wrap my legs around it as well, but there was nothing to keep me in place. I slipped roughly downward, badly scraping my skin through my jeans before I again got a toe hold and wedged my knee against the wood.

I could no longer hear the shots over the intensity of the water's rush.

A shadow suddenly blocked the little light I had as it loomed above me. It seemed somehow attached to the corner post of the railing directly over my head. Then it separated and fell past me, thudding below.

"Simon." His name died on my parted lips, as tears stung my eyes.

I could hear footsteps on the planks above. The gunman.

A hand on my calf startled me. Then, I, too, let go. I fell several feet on top of Simon, forcing a muffled curse from him along with the air from his lungs.

We had no time for him to recover. I dove forward, dragging two fistfuls of Simon's jacket with me, landing us both on a slab of smooth rock. We were under the lookout deck.

The moon slit its light through the spaces between the planks. For the first time since the first shot, we had the advantage. The shadow above us showed us exactly where our assailant stood.

Again, I drew out my gun, but Simon folded his hand over the barrel reflected in a sliver of light. One of his eyes was illuminated as well, and I watched as he held it trained for movement above.

I put my gun away. We were too far below. I couldn't hope to get a shot up through the narrow openings, and my gun wasn't powerful enough to drive through the wood. Shooting would only alert the person above to our location.

We held our breaths as the shooter circled the perimeter of the deck, the beam of a high powered flashlight sweeping the blackness. Then he broke and ran, his footsteps thudding hard against the wood. He'd have to find a safer way over the railing than the one we took. It would buy us at least a few minutes.

I pushed up against the cold surface of the rock. Simon was next to me. I reached a hand toward his shoulder and drew it back when I felt something wet.

"You're hurt," I said, leaning close enough so that he could hear my whisper.

"I'm all right. It's only a scratch. Rappelling without a rope is not a bright idea."

"Right. We call it falling."

"Isaacs is out there bleeding," I added.

I heard the sharp intake of his breath, even above the noise of the water. I wondered if it was from pain or worry over Isaacs.

"He's dead, isn't he?" I said. "And if he isn't, the

person who shot at us may go back and—"

"You're still the primary target. He'll take care of Isaacs later."

Simon was right. We had to find a way out from under the deck before our assailant found a way to us.

The shore was a jumble of boulders. We were stranded. The only way back that didn't include swimming the inlet was the way we'd come in, back over the wooden walkway. Not an option.

It took us precious seconds to feel our way over the boulders in the dark. I pulled myself into the moonlight with Simon right behind me. I was thankful to be out in the open but acutely aware that we were once again exposed.

We both drew our guns, but the going was still incredibly rough. I returned mine to my waist band. I needed both hands to steady myself, and I didn't want to lose my only weapon.

A stand of trees and bushes lay directly ahead of us. I led the way as we forced ourselves across the uneven rock as quickly as possible. We had to seek cover before our assailant returned. This time we wouldn't hear his footsteps on wood.

I turned and saw Simon lagging several feet behind me. I went back to him. His breathing was ragged, but even more alarming was the dark, spreading patch near his shoulder. A jolt of fear shot through me. Simon hadn't lost his handhold and fallen off the deck. He'd been shot. I forced myself to be calm. I pulled his left arm over my shoulder and grabbed him around the waist.

"Lean on me," I said.

He didn't argue as we hobbled as quickly as we could across the rough ground toward the darkness of the trees. We felt our way inside the copse, branches scraping at our faces and brush dragging at our legs. At least the vegetation had broken down some of the rock surface, making the going for our feet a little easier.

I had to know how badly Simon was wounded. That meant risking a look in the moonlight. I glanced over my shoulder. I could barely make out the sweep of a light beam in the distance through the trees. It would take our pursuer a few minutes to figure out which way we'd gone.

I steered Simon toward the inlet side of the tiny island. A boulder loomed just past the trees and I helped him around on the far side, easing him down to rest against it. The moonlight confirmed my worst fears. The round tear in Simon's leather jacket was unmistakable. So was the blood seeping from it. He was growing weaker, and I was afraid he might go into shock.

I unzipped his jacket and pulled it open. The wound needed pressure against it. I pulled off my own jacket and stripped off the long sleeved T-shirt I had on underneath.

He tugged on my arm and I leaned closer to hear what he had to say. "We really don't have time for that right now."

"Behave yourself or I'll stick this in your mouth instead of your wound," I warned.

I wadded the T-shirt into a ball and shoved it against the wound. Then I re-zipped his jacket over it. It was tight enough the leather should hold it in place. "We need to keep pressure on it," I said.

Shivering, I put back on my jacket and zipped it against the cool night air. I touched the back of my hand to Simon's cheek, his eyes glistening with pain in the moonlight. His skin was cool and too pale.

Suddenly memory flooded my mind.

Simon's handsome face. Laughing, charming. The immediate connection we'd felt in the bar, unlike anything I'd ever experienced. The feeling I'd known him half my life, the certainty that we shared some sort of mysterious bond. His ordering me a second beer. Wes's anger.

Then at Simon's house. Talking, touching, kissing him, shyly at first, then passionately. The two of us hungry for each other, reveling in the attraction. Drawing each other closer. Tumbling into his bed upstairs. Taking both my mind and body to places they had never been before. Then quiet contentment. The sweet kiss when we awakened the next morning.

I remembered it all. He took my breath away, just as he had the other two times we'd made love, only then there had been no fear, no distrust. No wonder Simon had been stunned when I told him of my amnesia.

"Are you all right?" he asked, claiming my hand.

I'd forgotten to breathe. "I'm fine," I assured him, forcing a smile and grateful for the darkness concealing the blush coloring my cheeks from having doubted him.

Simon coughed. It was getting harder for him to talk. "There's something I need to tell you."

"We don't have time," I told him. "If you haven't noticed, someone out there is trying to kill us."

I brushed my fingertips against his lips to quiet him. Then I took his head in my hands as I leaned down to give him one last kiss him before I left, desperately hoping it wouldn't be the last kiss we shared. His mouth responded but his strength was waning. Fighting tears, I dug my fingers into his thick, dark hair.

That's when I felt it—a large, rough patch of hairless skin hidden behind his right ear. An old head wound. A bad one.

I drew back, stunned as the truth hit me as though I'd had a blow to my head. How he wouldn't let me run my fingers through his hair, his knowledge of amnesia, his profession, the restored Mustang, his genuine pain at the mention of the Whitehalls, the reason Michael's family had refused a public funeral. *Why* Simon was here. The last piece of the puzzle that was Simon Talbot had instantly fallen into place.

But was it possible?

And Jesse's horrible lie.

Simon watched me, aware of what had just happened and daring me to say it out loud. My eyes swam as I searched his face, knowing, for the first time, exactly who he was.

His experiences had so altered him, I would never have suspected. The lovely, hopeful face of youth had hardened into something quite different. Still handsome, yet underneath it...

"Michael," I whispered, tears stinging my eyes.

He tried to push himself upright, but the pain pulled him back down.

"Yes," he managed.

A beam of light swept the branches above us. We didn't have time for him to explain.

"Jesse knows who you are," I whispered, pulling Simon's weapon from its holster and pressing it into his hand, hoping he'd have the strength to pull the trigger if it came to that.

I stood and drew my own gun from the waistband of my jeans.

"Eva, don't," Simon gasped, his words almost inaudible.

I didn't look back. I slipped into the darkness, already wishing I'd risked the time for one more kiss.

Chapter 18

My fight with Jesse Sedwick was personal. He had betrayed me in the worst possible way. Not only had he pretended to befriend me for years and then tried to kill me, he'd hurt Claire, one of the people I loved most in this world.

And he'd lied. About Simon. About everything. All of these years.

And now he'd made me responsible for endangering both Simon and Isaacs. How dare he?

Fury tensed my body and doubled my heart rate. I forced myself to breathe deeply and release my anger, as I steadied myself behind a tree trunk, my gun at the ready. There'd be plenty of time to hate later. Right now I had to keep my wits about me. I was on my own, I was outgunned, and, unlike Jesse, I had never shot anyone.

I promised myself I would not hesitate to take Jesse down. I had to remember everything Barry taught me. My compassion, he'd warned, was my worst enemy.

I'd known Jesse a lot of years. A part of me cared about him, or the man I'd thought he was. To pretend I didn't could get me killed. I cared even more for his wife Nina. The man who wanted to kill me was no longer some faceless monster in a Hummer trying to run me off the road. He was the man who had held my hand, vowed to protect me, and wiped my teenage tears.

Only Jesse wasn't really that man. That man had never existed. No, Jesse was the man behind the August Eight murders, the man who would now do whatever was necessary to keep his secrets hidden.

The hatred I felt swelled inside me again. I tamped it

down. Jesse would have figured out where Simon and I were by now. He would have first scoured the area under the observation deck, then the rocks leading down to the falls. We weren't foolish enough to try that path. One misstep and we would have wound up in the rushing waters of the Potomac. And if I was going to die tonight, I'd be damned if I was going to do it by tripping down some slope.

I had no intention of dying, at least not alone. My hand tightened around my pistol grip.

Jesse was near the front of the copse, searching the area with his flashlight. I held my breath as I waited for the beam to sweep past me to my left and then carefully stepped forward, making as much distance as possible before ducking behind another tree as the light cut back across. Once it had passed again, I traveled as quickly as I could until another swing of light stilled me. I was certain he would come into the woods. He had to know he'd hit Simon as he went over the railing of the observation deck.

The vegetation on this end of the tiny island was too dense for his light to do much good, but Jesse still had the advantage. We were surrounded on three sides by water, leaving us literally backed into a corner.

When Jesse finally spotted me, I wanted to be as far away from Simon as I could get, on the opposite edge of the water, the one near the falls. Simon was in no shape for a confrontation.

The beam of Jesse's flashlight suddenly disappeared. I stared into the darkness, waiting, but it didn't reappear. Could Jesse have given up and moved away? Again, I held my breath as I continued to watch, but I didn't see flashes of light anywhere.

No. He hadn't gone. He was using his night scope to search. It would be awkward and his field of vision would be limited, but I could no longer tell where he was.

I cursed. I'd lost the only advantage I'd had. I checked

my gun. I had the six bullets in the cylinder of my revolver and another round in my jacket pocket.

If I waited, Jesse might find Simon before he found me. I couldn't let that happen. I had to show myself. I plunged forward through the growth, brush tangling around my boots and grabbing at my pants legs, as I stumbled onto jagged rock in the moonlight. The water below rushed with incredible speed.

Quickly, I ducked down and a shot sped past my shoulder. He'd seen me. I found a low place, hoping to blend into the shadows created by the crevices.

I could hear Jesse moving toward me. He now knew exactly where I was. Which meant I had to move. I got down on my hands and knees and slipped back into the woods, staying right at the edge.

But Jesse was no fool. I could hear his movements, but I couldn't place him in the darkness. Until he spoke.

"Eva," he called out. "Eva is that you?"

He couldn't be more than twenty feet in front of me. Why would he locate himself for me? What sort of game was he playing? Did he actually believe I would be stupid enough to answer him?

"Are you all right?" he said. "I want to help you."

He was gambling that I hadn't figured it out, that I might think there was someone else in the park with us. But Jesse had underestimated me. And the connection I shared with Simon. Finding out Simon was actually Michael must have terrified him. He'd been forced to act before I found out, too.

I'd given him the perfect setup when I agreed to lure Simon and Isaacs to an isolated spot where he could take out all three of us and make it appear we'd shot each other. And, like an idiot, I'd gone along with it.

He hadn't killed Claire because she wasn't a threat to him. Indeed, he could use her injury to draw me out of hiding and to pressure me into letting him "protect" me.

But he wanted *me* dead. He knew I'd dig for the truth, and he wouldn't be able to wield the same influence now as he once had. As close as I was to the August Eight murders and as convinced as I was of Isaacs' guilt, I might discover something that would implicate Jesse. He was afraid that whatever frame he'd so carefully put together fifteen years ago might unravel if I looked closely enough.

For several seconds Jesse said nothing. I heard a branch snap, barely audible above the water. He'd moved closer. He was now several feet to my left.

I took in a deep breath and then expelled it, willing my anger to leave me as well. My hands felt sweaty inside my gloves, even in the cool night air.

All of Jesse's fatherly interest in the loved ones of the victims had been a carefully calculated plan to get close to us, to make us trust him so he could be certain that if any of us thought of anything that would point to him, he'd know it right away. Especially me. I was his selected witness, the one who could identify Isaacs' car, but who couldn't identify the person driving it.

I needed to move. He was getting too close. I ducked and rolled through the brush to the next tree. If I could somehow get behind him.... I'd have to wait until he was almost on top of me.

A twig broke close by. I jerked my head in that direction. I could barely make out his outline at the edge of a tree trunk. I took aim at a shadow and pulled the trigger. The shot exploded in my ears. Jesse's cry told me it had hit home.

I closed my eyes and swallowed back bile as my hands shook. I was afraid I might be sick. I lost two seconds I couldn't afford to lose.

Leaves crunched behind me, just as the butt of a gun slammed against the side of my head. I went down hard. My vision blacked out for a second and pain seared through my skull. I felt my gun twist out of my hand. It thudded a few feet away. Then Jesse lifted me with one fist wrapped around my throat and dragged me the few feet into the open, throwing me painfully onto the ground on my back, straddling me. His .44 magnum was pointed straight at my head, his left hand still around my neck.

"Ever the fool, aren't you, Eva?"

I hadn't hit him. His cry had only been a ploy.

I could hear the contempt in his voice. It was not just his contempt for me, but for honesty and decency, for what made us human. Jesse Sedwick wasn't human. He was a psychopath of the worst kind, the kind that walked among us pretending to be one of us.

All the hatred, all the resentment for my stolen life boiled inside of me. Jesse Sedwick had claimed his last victim. And it wasn't me.

I had no time. I bent my right knee to my chest and thrust my boot against his abdomen as I grabbed hold of his belt with both hands and pushed with all of my strength. Jesse flew over my head landing hard on his face at the rock's edge.

I rolled, ripped the kubotan from its snap on my jacket, and leapt forward to apply all my weight to one knee between his shoulder blades. But Jesse twisted beneath me, thrusting me backward. My back slammed against the base of a tree, knocking most of the air from my lungs.

He grabbed me again by my throat and practically lifted me off the ground, his hatred crushing the breath from me. I felt myself fading as he choked the life out of me, and spots speckled my vision. I only had seconds. I didn't hesitate. I did exactly what Barry had taught me. I rammed the end of the small baton straight into Jesse's temple. His body went limp. I gasped air back into my lungs as his hand dragged down my chest and he fell against my legs.

I pushed him back and scrambled away, frantically searching for my revolver. I found it a few feet away, glinting in the moonlight. I trained it on Jesse, but he didn't move.

"Jesse," I whispered.

He didn't respond. I inched forward. He was lying face up. Both of his eyes and his mouth were open. He didn't seem to be moving. Cautiously I reached my hand toward his face. I felt no air coming from his nose or his mouth. I'd hoped to knock Jesse unconscious, but my fingers pressed against his carotid artery told me otherwise.

I backed away to the edge of the rock, horrified, the waters of the Potomac rushing angrily below me. Clutching my revolver against my chest, I collapsed as my body shuddered from what I'd just done.

Chapter 19

"Take that look off of your face, Eva. Look at the man. He's sleeping like a baby. He's going to be fine," Wilma insisted, patting the back of my hand as I held Simon's. I was sitting in a chair I'd pulled up next to his hospital bed, watching him breathe. In the twenty minutes I'd been there, he had yet to stir.

The doctor had assured me that Simon's surgery had gone well and that I had no need to worry. Nothing vital had been hit and they'd extracted the bullet without any complications. But he'd lost a lot of blood, and had to have two transfusions. He'd be weak and very sore for a while, but he should heal rapidly, considering what good shape he was in. Still, I couldn't relax until Simon opened his eyes and told me himself that he was all right.

I'd spent most of the night at the police station being grilled by two detectives who thought Jesse Sedwick walked on water. But Jesse wasn't the only one with friends in the police department. They'd rushed the ballistics tests. The bullets fired from Jesse's rifle matched the one recovered from Al's body and would soon match the ones that had been dug out of Simon and Isaacs. As bizarre as my story must have sounded, the evidence didn't lie.

"Stop blaming yourself," Wilma said, stirring me from my thoughts. "Jesse can have all the blame for himself."

"But I devised the plan that almost got us killed."

"Pish. You thought you were helping the police bring in two fugitives."

I opened my mouth.

She held up her hand. "I'm not listening to one more

word. You feel guilty that Simon and Isaacs were shot. And you feel guilty for killing Jesse. You shouldn't. Remember what he did. You told me yourself. He killed seven people to hide Michael's murder, not counting my Al. And he was willing to kill both you and Simon and pin it on Isaacs to keep you from uncovering the truth. You were damn lucky his plan didn't succeed."

"But will we ever have proof of why he wanted Michael—Simon—dead to begin with?" I asked.

"Maybe not. But Jesse had to have been the one to set up the ambush of the witness that testified against Paul O'Brien. Someone made sure there were two rookie cops in that cruiser and two armed men waiting to take them out. It almost had to be someone in the department."

"Jesse admitted he put Michael on that detail when I interviewed him."

"That was probably a slip on his part, one he wanted to make sure never became part of your documentary."

"And if Michael hadn't 'died' in the August murder spree..."

"He would have figured out that Jesse was behind it all. So there would have been some other unfortunate accident befalling one Michael Whitehall before he completely recovered."

"But the overkill of the drive-by shootings..." I shuddered again at the thought. "Wilma, how could anyone justify that, even to himself, if Michael was the only real target?"

"That I don't know, baby cakes. But Jesse was determined his role in both crimes would not come out. He was afraid of you and your documentary."

I swallowed hard. All I'd wanted was justice. Now that I had it, why wasn't I satisfied?

Simon's eyes fluttered open. "Hey."

"Hey, yourself."

He tried to smile but the anesthesia and the painkillers had left his muscles so relaxed, he could barely lift the corners of his mouth. He licked his lips.

I grabbed up the cup of water on his bedside table and offered it to him. He took a long sip through the straw.

"I take it this isn't heaven," he said, handing me back the cup.

"What gave it away?" I asked.

"Your clothes. I would have hoped you'd be in something filmy and see-through, like gossamer."

I looked down. I was truly a mess. My jeans and jacket were bloodied and torn. But I'd refused to go home and wash up before I knew for myself that Simon was all right.

"And me," Wilma piped up. "Don't think I'd be in Simon's version of heaven."

He winked at her. "Right at the center of it, Wilma."

She beamed. "I'm going to step outside and give you two some time alone."

As soon as the door shut behind her, I felt Simon's grip tighten and saw the strength return to his eyes. "You had no choice. You do know that, don't you?"

I nodded. Simon had been barely conscious when I finally managed to get myself up and back through the trees to tell him what had happened. Intellectually I knew what he was saying was true, but emotionally I was having problems with Jesse's death. I thought I was prepared to kill in self-defense, but it wasn't something I'd ever really expected to have to do. I knew the devastation death wreaked and I wanted no part of it. Nina had been on my mind throughout the night, almost as much as Simon.

"I'm so sorry I didn't trust you," I whispered. "I almost got you killed."

"You almost got us both killed," he corrected.

My whole body went rigid.

He smiled and took my hand, his grip surprisingly

strong. "You *saved* my life."

I paused, willing the constriction in my throat to relax. "Simon...Michael...I don't know what to call you."

"Simon's fine. I've been Simon for a lot years."

"Why that name?"

"If my parents had had a second son, he would have been Simon."

"They named you?"

"As though I'd been born again."

That surprised me, but Simon's head wound had been very serious. He wouldn't have been able to make any decisions for himself for a good while.

"And Talbot?" I asked.

Simon fumbled for the controls to his bed. I handed them to him and he raised the head of his bed before he reclaimed my hand. He was much more alert than he'd been moments before.

"My father picked it at random out of the phone book. He didn't want anyone to be able to trace me in any way. He had all the paperwork filled out to legally change my name. It was ready for me to sign when I was well enough to be told what was going on."

It blew my mind. One of the August Eight had survived. How ironic was it that he was the only one who had been specifically targeted.

"So they created a new identity for you," I said. "How could they do that?"

"My dad had a friend who was with the FBI. A death certificate was faked, and my dad had me secretly transported to a private hospital in Pittsburgh. I was in rehab for months. I don't know all the details, but it's legal."

"They told the press you had died."

"And all my relatives and friends."

"Your parents continued to live here in Maryland."

"Dad said they didn't dare move."

"They must have loved you a lot."

"They did."

"And you loved them enough to go along with it."

I was sure that was the only reason he'd agreed to it. He smiled and I thought I detected a wince.

"Are you in pain?" I asked.

He shook his head. "Whatever they gave me is working really fine."

"You have to be exhausted."

"I bet I've had more rest than you."

That was true. But I was still running on adrenaline and I wanted answers to some of my questions.

"So no one else knows who you are."

"No one but my chief in Pittsburgh."

"Your father believed whoever went on that killing spree wanted you dead."

"He thought it likely."

"Who did he suspect?"

"I lost three months of my memories, pretty much everything after my graduation from the academy. So Jesse succeeded in suppressing whatever information I had that might point to him. My father didn't know who was behind the murders or what I might have known, but he was too good a cop to believe that a police officer involved in a shooting and on administrative leave like I was would just happen to be the first in a line of random murders."

"I assume the investigation into who could have leaked the time and route for transporting the witness never went anywhere," I said.

"Jesse covered his tracks well. I'm sure O'Brien paid him a small fortune for that information."

"Why didn't you just tell me who you were when we first met?" I asked.

He squeezed my hand as he looked me straight into my eyes. "Because I didn't trust you."

His words stung. But why should he have trusted me?

As I studied his face, I began to suspect it had nothing to do with me. Simon Talbot, born at the instant of Michael Whitehall's death, probably didn't trust anyone except his mother and his father, and they'd been dead for years. Someone he'd known *and trusted* as a rookie cop—Jesse—had tried to kill him, and he'd had no idea who that someone was for years.

"I should go and let you rest," I said. I started to stand, but the grip he had on my hand wouldn't let me move.

"I don't want you to go."

"But I'm not good at being quiet. There's so much I want to ask you."

"Then ask. I'll throw you out when I'm too tired."

I didn't believe that for a minute.

"You've been working with Isaacs and Christopher, haven't you?" I asked. "Why?"

"You were gunning for Isaacs."

I felt a rush of guilt as the why suddenly fell into place. "You came here to protect him from me."

"I couldn't let him be victimized again, especially when the real killer had never been caught. Jesse had pounded Isaacs' guilt into your head and everyone else's who would listen for years, and he kept it up the whole time you were working on the documentary."

"Even as you cast doubt on it. That must have really irritated him. But how did you know Isaacs wasn't behind the murders?"

"I told you, Eva, I've been looking into this case for fifteen years. Isaacs is no psychopath. It takes one heartless son-of-a-bitch to kill eight people, seven of them random, in a murder spree. Isaacs wasn't your man."

But Jesse was.

"That day when we left the hospital and Christopher was following us—"

"I knew you would spot the car, so I had to make him first. I didn't want you to suspect at that point that I knew him. Of course, I didn't actually expect you to get his license plate number."

"And Manny, your buddy who ran Christopher's plate for you?"

"He's was just giving me information I already knew. But I did go by to see Christopher's mother like you asked me to. She was every bit as crazy as I told you. By the way, how is Isaacs?"

"They patched him up, but they didn't admit him. Christopher took him home to Mary Ann's."

I shook my head thinking of Isaacs, who had taken two bullets that were meant for me. He needed me alive to clear him. Another irony when I was so intent on getting him convicted.

After I'd killed Jesse, I'd lain on the rock in the moonlight, wondering if I'd ever be able to get up. I don't know how much time passed before I finally pushed myself up and dragged myself back through the trees. When I'd gotten back to Simon, I'd found him weak and close to shock. I'd called the police on his cell phone and asked for three ambulances. Then I made it back to the area in front of the tavern to find Isaacs and wait for help to arrive, so I could direct them to where Simon was.

I found Isaacs lying on the pavement, holding his injured arm. Amazingly, he'd been able to stop the bleeding. I'd expected him to hate me, but he just seemed glad neither of us was dead.

"Hey, look at me."

Simon reached over and turned my chin in his direction.

"Don't be sad. We made it out alive, Eva. And you've got your ending. You can finish your documentary."

I tried to smile. I did have my ending, but it wasn't the one I'd expected.

Chapter 20

"Are you sure you want to film him right now?" Ben asked in my ear, hoping Isaacs wouldn't hear as he assessed his subject. "He's kind of banged up."

"Right here, right now. I want every bruise, every bandage, every scratch on film. We've been beating this man up for fifteen years. I want everyone to see what Jesse Sedwick and the rest of us did to him."

Ben took another light reading on Isaacs' face as he sat in Simon's swivel desk chair. I'd positioned him so that Ben would catch the photos of Jackie's father and Claire's sister in the wide frame. I would be off camera for the interview. I didn't want my presence to distract from the impact of what Isaacs had been through.

"I want you to get a slow pan of the room before you focus in on him," I told Ben.

I wanted the photos, the timelines, the descriptions and information on each of the victims, all written in bold black marker on white paper, to hit the viewer full force, just as they had me the first time I'd stepped into this room. This was what we'd all lost.

And now I wanted Isaacs to tell us what he'd lost.

I sat down on top of Simon's desk, and Ben gave me a cue to let me know he was ready to roll.

"Tell me what happened that morning in August when the police came to your door."

I listened as Isaacs told of his confusion and disbelief. Of being so out of it from drugs and alcohol, he'd had no idea why the police were there. Of how Jesse had almost convinced him that he must have killed those people and stolen those goods in the trunk of his car. How he didn't remember anything that had happened the night before. How he'd fallen into a nightmare from which he'd never awakened. How he'd had faith, someday, all of it would end.

Four hours later, we were all exhausted. Isaacs moved to stand up.

"I have a couple of more questions, if you don't mind," I said.

"Sure. I thought we were done," Isaacs said.

"Before the shootings, had you ever met Detective Sedwick?"

"He'd arrested me a couple of times."

"So he knew your habits, about your drug use, where you lived, that you lived alone, and how you spent your evenings."

He nodded. "Drunk and high. That was pretty much everything there was to know about me."

"Ben, could you please turn off the camera."

"You don't want the rest of this on tape?" Ben asked.

"No. You can go ahead and start packing up."

I would not hurt this man again by recording anything that might be used as evidence against him.

"Did Jesse ever try to recruit you to help him with anything illegal?"

Isaacs looked me straight in the eye. "I've done a lot of bad things in my life, but I never did more than steal."

"And you never worked with anyone else, not even to fence merchandise?"

"No, ma'am. It was always just the two of us. Me and the drugs."

"Did you know Paul O'Brien," I asked.

"I've never heard of him."

"Thanks, Luther," I said.

"This documentary you're making...are a lot of people gonna to see it?"

"Lots," I promised.

"And the ones who do, they're all gonna know I'm innocent?"

I swallowed back my guilt. "Every one of them."

While Ben loaded up our gear, I helped Isaacs out to the car he'd borrowed from Mary Ann and thanked him again. He'd insisted that Christopher not come to the taping. He didn't think he could say what he needed to with him in the room. I'd agreed. I would interview Christopher as well, but later. Isaacs was fine with that. This was every bit as much their story as it was ours.

"You coming?" Ben asked, startling me from the doorway dividing the kitchen from the living room. I'd gone back inside after Isaacs left and sat down in Simon's chair to stare at the walls as I'd seen him do many times.

"You go ahead," I said. "I'm going to sit here for a while."

"I don't like the sound of that."

I offered Ben a half smile. "I'm fine. I'd tell you if I wasn't."

"Really?"

"Yeah, really. Now get yourself out of here. I'll bet you've got plans for tonight."

"Me, Wes, and some of the boys are catching a few beers."

"Then go catch one for me."

"Will do."

I was still angry with Wes, but I knew I had no right to be. He'd only been relaying Al's message to me, a message that turned out to be true.

"Don't stay here too long," Ben added.

"I won't. Simon's expecting me this evening. He hates hospital food. Question is how am I going to sneak in prime rib?"

"Lots of tin foil," Ben suggested. "When's he getting out?"

"About ten o'clock tomorrow morning. I'm taking him back to my house to recuperate."

"Lucky man. Are the repairs finished?"

"Are you kidding me? I'm lucky to have the plywood up."

"You think it's safe to stay there with no alarm system?"

"Safer than staying here with no system," I assured him.

"If you get spooked—"

"I'll call you. Thanks, Ben. Don't forget we have the second interview with Debra Roddy scheduled for tomorrow afternoon."

"I've got it on my calendar."

"Good. Oh, and do me a favor, Ben," I added. "Send a copy of the video we did of Isaacs to our producer when you get a chance. I think he's going to be pleased with what we got today."

"Sure." He paused. "You want to talk about it?"

"About what?"

"What's bothering you."

It hadn't escaped Ben that in the time we we'd been talking, I hadn't been able to take my eyes from the photos and papers lining the walls.

"I'm all right. I just need to be in this room a little while longer. Pull the back door shut, and please lock it when you leave."

A few minutes later I heard the van pull out of the drive. The sun was going down, and it was getting colder again as I continued to sit and stare at the walls.

Why, Jesse? Why so many?

What could he have been thinking? Every death multiplied the chances of getting caught. Every shot risked more witnesses. Why eight when four would have been more than enough to confuse the authorities?

Jesse hadn't killed Claire when he so easily could have. Had his blood lust diminished over the years? Or was I missing something?

I stood and went to the map Simon had taped near the doorframe. The location of each shooting was circled in black and marked with the time that it had occurred. I traced the path. First Michael. Then Claire's sister, April Bennett, one street over. Further down on the corner of that same street, David Harrison, leaving me as an eyewitness.

My finger lingered on the spot. I'd never gone back there, certain to this day, that I'd see the stain of David's blood on the sidewalk. I'd have to face it soon. I intended to film it.

I forced my hand onward. Another two streets over Jackie's father, Horace Gonzalez, had died. Then two streets skipped before Karen Durwood, in the middle of the block, followed by Edwina Jackson on the next street. Dennis Toro near the church around the next corner. And the last, Sabrina Tyler, at the community center. A clear, straight path of dots almost equally spaced.

If not less, then why not more? Why had Jesse stopped when he did? My finger continued to tap against the map as the answer suddenly became clear.

My God. Why hadn't I seen it before?

Chapter 21

"You're sure you're up to this?" I asked Simon as I pulled his baby blue Mustang as close to my front door as my driveway would allow.

"Doc says I'll be fine as long as you promise to take good care of me. I was thinking maybe you could get one of those cute little candy striper outfits."

"Me in pink and white stripes? Never gonna happen."

"Okay. Black leather works, too. I guess that means a bell to summon you whenever I need you is probably a no go."

"Right on your first guess."

He wouldn't need a bell or anything else to call me. I planned to never be more than a couple of steps away while he was recuperating.

I climbed out of the car, came around, and opened the passenger door. I didn't particularly like his coloring. The short trip from the hospital had already tired him out.

"You sure you're ready for this?" I asked.

"As ready as you are."

Simon pushed himself up, braced against me, and pulled himself out of the car. His left arm was in a sling to help immobilize his shoulder. He leaned against me as I helped him onto the concrete stoop where I steadied him and unlocked the front door.

I pushed the door inward. It was dark and quiet inside. I again positioned Simon's right arm back across my shoulders as we moved forward.

"We're heading right. I'm putting you in my bed," I directed, as I steered him.

"I like the sound of that."

"I thought you would."

Carefully, I eased him onto the bed. Then I grabbed a couple of extra pillows from the top shelf in the closet and positioned them behind him. He sank back against their softness.

"You rest," I ordered. "I'm going to make us some lunch."

"You're going to cook?"

"Of course. Right after I put on my candy striper outfit."

He was waiting for me when I crossed into the kitchen, sitting in the same chair Simon had been in when I'd come home early Monday morning.

"Scream and I'll blow you away."

Wes's finger tightened around the trigger of a .38 special equipped with a silencer.

"I'm not going to scream, Wes. We've known each other a lot of years. I think the least we can do is have a civil conversation before you kill me."

My calm disturbed him. The least he'd expected was surprise and rage. What he'd hoped for was fear. But I refused to give him anything he wanted. Nor would I let him see the hatred inside of me. Not yet.

Last night my anger had exploded at Simon's. I'd ripped everything off the walls when I realized Wes must have been driving Isaacs' car that night. Jesse would never have risked killing those people himself, not when he had an eager psychopath to do the job, one he had known and mentored throughout his teenage years.

The answer had been there on Simon's walls all along. The path on the map led to the name of the shooter, the boyfriend who couldn't resist flaunting his power over life and death in Sabrina's face.

There'd been two intended victims that night: Simon

and Sabrina, one at the beginning of the string and the other at the end.

"So you went out drinking with Ben last night," I said. "He told you that I'd be bringing Simon here this morning, and that my alarm system wasn't functional."

"Ben's not so bright. Get a couple of beers in him, and you can't shut him up. He told me he was worried about you. He actually thinks of me as a friend."

So had I at one time.

"What did you do to Ben that made him sick last week? You put something in his food or his beer when the two of you went out, so I'd have to let you work for me."

"I needed to find out what you were planning, how much information you were getting. Jesse was getting nervous."

I felt a new surge of resentment shoot through me. Ben deserved better.

My eyes narrowed as I took in the features of a killer. I'd tried to be Wes's friend. I'd defended the bastard to most of the people we'd both known over the years. I'd identified with him. We were the two who had lost our young loves that night, only his love for Sabrina was even more of a sham than my feelings for David. I'd been convinced Sabrina's death had made Wes into the self-centered, irresponsible creature that he was. How wrong I'd been.

"I've got most of what you and Jesse did figured out, but not quite all. You were really clever."

The self-satisfied curl to his lip told me my flattery had worked. He couldn't resist telling me. He wanted me to know before I died.

"When Jesse mapped out what he wanted you to do that night in August fifteen years ago, he didn't tell you to kill eight people, did he?" I asked.

"Three. Four max."

"Right. Just enough so Michael's death would look like

it was part of a drive-by shooting spree, maybe a gang initiation. And, of course, you'd have to leave an eyewitness to describe Isaacs' car.

"But you had no idea the kind of high you'd get from murder," I went on.

I could see the excitement dance in his eyes at the memory. Killing me would be sweet, but nothing like the power he'd experienced that night.

"And you were angry with Sabrina. You knew she'd gone to that dance without you when you'd told her not to. She was trying to break away from you, and you didn't like that. You knew she'd be taking smoke breaks. You wanted her to see you, didn't you, even if she didn't know it was you. When she heard about the killings the next day on the news, you wanted her to remember seeing the car, to know that the murder spree had come right to her, to realize that she could have been a victim that night. You wanted her scared of you. You wanted her to know the power you had over her.

"But when you saw her, she wasn't alone. She was a beautiful girl. There were boys around her. You were so angry you wanted to add her to the list. And why not, no one would ever suspect. And she'd goaded you into it. You stopped and waited until she stepped away from the group so you could get a clear shot. Then you killed her before anyone could realize where the shot had come from."

It was more probable that he had every intention of killing her all along. That was why he'd taken so many lives. Leave a gap in the string of deaths, and Sabrina's death would stand out, immediately bringing motives for her murder into question. I'd given him the alternate possibility, hoping he would correct me, hoping I could finally get him talking.

"I don't want to talk about Sabrina."

His gun shifted and his eyes hardened. I knew I was on shaky ground.

"Okay. Would you like to talk about being the second

shooter in the ambush of the cruiser which was transporting the witness to the Paul O'Brien trial?"

"You know about that?"

I could see sweat forming on Wes's forehead. He hadn't expected me to have figured that out.

"Jesse and I had some time at the park to talk before he died," I lied.

"He wouldn't have told you that. If he had, you would have already had the police on my tail."

"What'd he do?" I asked. "Did he blackmail you or were you partners?"

"Shut up."

"Was he grooming you all those years you were in and out of juvenile hall, or did he have evidence against you that he intended to use if you didn't go along with what he wanted you to do?"

"I said shut up."

"You owed him," I pressed. "And he offered you the chance for a good deal of money. Only you botched the job. You killed Rhodes, but when Michael got out of the car and started shooting, you took off."

"Are you calling me a coward?"

Wes's eyes turned even meaner, and, for a moment, I was afraid I'd overplayed my hand.

"No." I kept my voice low and soothing. "If I were you, I would have run, too. Your partner was dead, the courthouse was only a couple of miles away, the police would be there any minute. What choice did you have?"

Wes's posture relaxed slightly.

"But you wanted revenge. You didn't get paid, and now Jesse had an even bigger hold over you. You had to make it right. And you wanted Michael dead every bit as much as Jesse and O'Brien.

"Jesse wanted Michael dead because he would eventually trace his assignment to transport the witness who was to testify against O'Brien back to him. O'Brien wanted him dead because the witness's testimony convicted him. You wanted him dead because he'd made you feel like a fool."

"I'm no fool."

"I know you're not."

"Neither are you. I told Jesse he should just let me take you out instead of trying to do it himself. But he wanted Isaacs dead at the same time, so he could somehow pin your death on him. He needed me to set it all up, to get Isaacs and you together in the alley next to the bar. Only Simon messed things up by showing up at the bar Saturday night."

Finally. He was talking. All I needed was a little more.

"So you tried again Sunday night. It was you in the Hummer that ran me off the road, wasn't it?"

The rage that had been behind that attack had to have come from someone like Wes. He was a different kind of psychopath from Jesse, one who didn't care if he ever fit into society. Jesse was amoral. For him, killing was simply taking care of business. With Wes it was power.

"Did you steal the Hummer or did Jesse get it for you?"

"I did. I knew what I needed for the job. We figured you'd come looking for me sooner or later when I didn't answer your phone calls. I staked out my apartment, and I was right."

"Which one of you killed Al?"

"He came up behind Jesse while he was shooting at you in the alley. You can thank Al for saving your life. In the seconds that it took for Jesse to deal with him, you got away."

I felt tears threaten my eyes, but I was determined Wes wouldn't see any of my weakness. Again, I tamped down my anger. I needed full command of my body.

"So you're here to finish me off."

"You and that bastard in your bed."

Wes was still possessive of me, as he'd been throughout the years. He wanted control over me, the same kind of control he'd wanted over Sabrina, and he resented any man who might have a place in my life.

I nodded. "Want some juice? I've got some oj and maybe some V8."

"Are you kidding me?"

I pulled open the refrigerator door and spun, pulling my revolver from the back of my jeans, the door shielding my body.

"No, I'm not kidding you, you sick bastard." My rage surged.

"You don't have it in you," Wes taunted, his body tensing. "See, that's the difference between us. You don't want me dead."

He was exposed now. I had the advantage.

"Put down your gun, Wes. I'm a dead shot. Are you willing to bet your life that I'm not?"

"I'm willing to bet you didn't mean to kill Jesse. And, sweetheart, we had a lot more between us than you and Jesse ever did."

"Is that right?" a male voice asked.

Simon stood in the doorway, holding the gun he'd brought into the house in his sling.

In the second it took for Wes's eyes to shift in Simon's direction, I stepped out and shot his arm, dead into the muscle that controls hand movement.

Wes watched in horror as his fingers loosened and the gun began to fall.

"Uh-uh," I warned as he made a grab toward the gun with his left hand. I slammed the refrigerator door.

"Don't give me a reason to take out your other hand. You'll need one to sign your confession."

Wes raised his chin, a defiant sneer on his mouth. "What confession? It's your word against mine. I'll say you killed Jesse and then tried to frame me. I'll tell them you asked me to come here to talk to you about your film and then forced me to put my fingerprints on that weapon. It's untraceable and it hasn't even been fired."

"Sort of like what you and Jesse did with Isaacs? You stole the goods and helped Jesse press Isaacs' fingerprints on them before putting them in the trunk of his car."

"Something like that. The police aren't going to buy your story, not without proof."

"Then I guess we'll have to give them some."

"Give them what?" Wes spat out. "If you'd had any proof you would have taken it to the police."

I nodded toward the large dish garden sitting on top of my refrigerator that I'd bought in the hospital gift shop. And a second one on the bookcase along the side wall. There were two more in my bedroom, in case Wes had tried to ambush me there.

"You know I don't keep plants. I always kill them. You're on camera, Wes, and so is your full confession. It'll make one hell of a finish for my documentary."

Chapter 22

Time stops as the rusted Ford Fairlane with the puttied fender looms toward us. A gun barrel pokes through the open window, and fear rushes through me like an electric shock.

My sundress flares as I spin in slow motion to push my companion out of the line of fire. But just as I touch him, a blinding blast bursts between us, and we are both falling…falling…

"No!" strangled incoherently in my throat as I sat straight up in bed, clutching the sheet against my chest and gasping, as sweat streamed down my face.

"Shhhh. It's all right. You're here with me," Simon soothed. He cradled me against him, his strong arms encircling me, keeping me safe from my demons.

"Which one was it this time?" he asked, brushing the hair away from my face.

"David," I choked.

Sometimes I dreamt I was in the woods at Great Falls again, Jesse stalking me while Simon lay dying. I had to fight him again. In my dreams, I didn't always win.

Simon drew back enough to tilt my chin, so he could kiss away my tears. The gunshot wound to his shoulder had healed, but the scar was still pink. I realized I was lying on it and started to pull away.

"Hey, it's all right," he insisted. "I don't feel a thing."

I pressed against him, wanting nothing more than to be as close as possible to the one man who understood my personal hell. I wanted to be nowhere in this world more than exactly where I was—in Simon's arms.

I snuggled even closer, trying to block out the image of Wes's face leering at me out of the darkness. I had to keep reminding myself he would never hurt me or anyone else again.

"It's been two months since your last nightmare. That's pretty much a record for you."

I nodded against his arm. For more than fifteen years I'd had nightmares at least once a week. Now the dark figures in my dreams had faces. Maybe that should have made them less scary. But it didn't. But being with Simon had made their visits less frequent. And I could now hope that one day they'd go away all together. Maybe when Wes was convicted.

I knew now exactly why Wes treated me as though I owed him. He'd let me live that night when he killed David. In his mind, he'd saved my life. And, I guess, in some twisted way, he had. I'd never thought of surviving that night as a gift—until now. Until Simon.

"If you don't get some sleep, you'll have bags under those beautiful eyes of yours at the screening tomorrow."

I sighed. The documentary was finally finished. I was pleased with it, but it was a hard piece to watch, especially for those of us who had lived through it. Simon, however, seemed to be able to view it with surprising detachment. In a very real way, Michael *had* died that night. What Simon had sought to avenge was not Michael's death so much as the effect it had had on his family. And, of course, there was Luther Isaacs.

He'd become somewhat of a celebrity. Ironic, that this little man had to endure fifteen tormented years before anyone, other than Mary Ann and Christopher, cared about him. If Jesse hadn't pinned the murders on him, he'd most likely be dead from alcohol and drug abuse. Life does take some interesting turns.

"Have you decided which offer to go with?"

I shook my head. Several cable networks and one national network had expressed interest in purchasing the documentary. My agent was brokering the deal. A lot of money was riding on their reaction to the film at the screening.

"I don't care who buys it. All I want is for it to be sold—gone—out of my hands and my mind."

"And I want Wes convicted," I added.

"He will be, thanks to you."

Then maybe my memory of that August night might finally be put to rest.

"It's time, Eva. You have to let it go. You've been living every day like it could be your last. You can't. You have to believe that there's a tomorrow."

I did believe it, thanks to Simon.

"I'm not giving up my motorcycle," I insisted.

"No one said you had to."

"And I'm still carrying my gun."

"You wouldn't be you without a little extra weight in the pocket of your leather jacket."

I smiled at him. "I'm never going to be completely normal. You know that, don't you?"

"I wouldn't have you any other way."

I laughed and snuggled closer. For the first time in my adult life, I was truly happy.

ACKNOWLEDGEMENTS

Thanks, once again, to the talented people who surround me and not only encourage my writing, but make it possible for me to do it. I especially would like to thank my husband and my daughters for their input and artistic skills. Pat Gagne, Robyn Amos, Elaine English, Ann Kline, Edie Claire, Natashya Wilson, and Charles Griemsman for their input into this book. And lastly, I would like to thank you, my readers, who buy my books and enjoy my work.

Visit Judy Fitzwater's web page at www.judyfitzwater.com

Contact her at judyfitzwater@gmail.com

"Like" her page on Facebook: Judy Fitzwater Author

OTHER BOOKS BY JUDY FITZWATER:

The Jennifer Marsh Mysteries:
Dying to Get Published
Dying to Get Even
Dying for a Clue
Dying to Remember
Dying to be Murdered
Dying to Get Her Man
Dying Before "I Do" (coming in 2014)

Suspense:
No Safe Place

Paranormal Romantic Comedy:
Vacationing with the Dead

CPSIA information can be obtained
at www.ICGtesting.com
Printed in the USA
LVHW110047040221
678346LV00011B/237